Confessions of
a Polish Used Car
Salesman

Confessions of a Polish Used Car Salesman

a novel by

Mark Wisniewski

1997   Hi Jinx Press,   Davis

Acknowledgements

The author would like to thank the editors of the following magazines, in which excerpts from this novel originally appeared: *Asylum, Bakunin, Colorado-North Review, Confrontation, Nexus, The Northern Review, Painted Hills Review.*

ISBN 1-57650-069-1
Library of Congress Catalog Number 97-071245

Hi Jinx Press
PO Box 1814
Davis, California 95617

For those beyond the bluebirds

Confessions of
a Polish Used Car
Salesman

The Decal

I grew up believing families were grandparents and kids, with nothing in between.

My grandmother was four foot ten. My grandfather kept *Playboys* and naked mannequins in the garage, on the rafters where my grandmother couldn't see them.

My grandmother could out-talk an auctioneer. My grandfather spoke nine words a day but had a twitch that got his point across.

Their Polish marriage was rock solid.

But then my grandmother met the Indian Lady.

The Indian Lady was bigger than my grandfather, and not just taller, either. I'm not sure she was full-blooded Indian, but she had caramel-colored skin and eyes black as wet licorice drops.

The Indian Lady would visit my grandmother on Tuesday afternoons. They'd sit at the cluttered kitchen table and exchange coupons. The Indian Lady sat with her legs apart, but it didn't matter.

One Tuesday afternoon I went to the bathroom. The bathroom was next to the kitchen: it had been a pantry when outhouses were legal. It still smelled like *kielbasa* spices and dill weed but now contained a sink, a bathtub, a portable electric whirlpool for arthritis, and a toilet.

Matted pink fur stained by liniment and shaving soap protected the toilet tank. The toilet lid had foreign coins in it, stuck there. The linoleum floor was egg-yolk yellow with gold specks shaped like corn flakes. I used to scratch the specks off and keep them in a matchbox, until my grandmother waxed them over.

The Tuesday I went to the bathroom, the specks were twelve waxings under: for eyes only, like money in cash registers.

So after I closed the door, I went to the bathroom the way

my grandmother did: sit down, face straight ahead, maybe look at the little lady.

The little lady was on the clothes chute door. She had orange hair and was naked except for a pair of high heels and a blue hand towel. One of her hands pressed the towel against her chest. The other covered the little space where her legs met. She had pink skin, smiling eyes, and red lips shaped like a tiny cherry Life Saver.

"*Oops!*" she was saying.

I wasn't sure why.

"You got doubles on ten cents off puffed rice?" a lady's voice said—the Indian Lady's.

Christ, I thought. Her again.

"No," my grandmother's voice said.

"Why sure you do. You threw it back in your Dutch Masters box."

"This here one?"

"No. The other. The Panatela one."

"Ten cents puffed rice? My bifocals. You see bifocals anywheres?"

"In the Panatela one. On top the ten cents puffed rice."

"Jesus. The other day I lost them on my nose. Aging everyday, I am."

"You don't need two ten cents puffed rice. Limit one is it?"

"Limit one. Expires the turdieth. But nineteen fifty-eight? Almost a year expired. Where'd that gosh-darn kid put my trash bag?"

I smiled at the little lady. She was a nice stranger: older than me but younger than anyone I knew, keeping her feet warm with high heels while drying her pink skin with a hand towel. Part of the towel was scratched away. I'd never noticed that before.

The nickel-colored doornob squeaked and turned. I slapped the opening door closed with my palm.

"Hide your shoo-shoo," my grandmother's voice said.

I squeezed my thighs together. For double protection I crammed my fist in the space where my legs met. The door opened: my grandmother, wearing her homemade dress and see-through plastic apron, looking at me through the magic halves of her silver bifocals. I thought: Could those things make your eyes any bigger?

"Hidden?" she asked.

I nodded two little ones. The Indian Lady could have seen me but was reading a Quaker Oats coupon colored like the American flag. Her legs were apart, her stockings rolled down to her knees. Her stockings were orange and shiny, not like my grandmother's sparrow-brown ones.

Indian stockings, I thought. The house smelled like meat pies. I looked at the waxed-over gold specks.

"You scratch that?" my grandmother said.

"What."

"*Look* at Grandma when she talks to you."

I looked at the bifocals. They were aimed at the little lady. My grandmother was pointing at the blue towel.

"You scratch this decal?"

I'd never heard the word "decal." Must be Polish, I thought. "Decal?"

My grandmother's swollen finger covered the little lady's navel. "*Decal.* Did you scratch it hey?"

I shook my head a slow one.

My grandmother glanced as far over her shoulder as her arthritis would allow. "He denies it."

I pressed my fist against my thighs and looked at the Indian Lady. She could have seen my underpants rubberbanded around my knees but was too busy stuffing my grandmother's coupons under her armpit. Her legs were still open. "Kids," she said.

My grandmother grabbed my chin and aimed it at her bifocals. "Then who scratched it, smart one?"

"Grandpa," I said, pronouncing it as it's spelled.

My grandmother's eyes grew closer: bigger.

"The stinker," The Indian Lady said. She was looking at the kitchen gadgets my grandfather had bought second hand. Daisy-shaped refrigerator magnets were halfway to the floor. Rusty colanders, jammed nut grinders, shorted-out hotplates and bent electric carving knives were piled cabinet-high on the counter. Someday my grandfather would fix them. Someday my grandmother would auction the doubles to neighbors. She'd get twice what he paid for them. They'd be rich.

The Indian Lady dropped a refrigerator magnet into her purse. My grandmother grabbed a half bar of gold Dial soap from the slimy Shell Station ash tray. It squirted from her hand like a bluegill. She girdled her stomach flab with one hand, bent over, picked up the soap. It had hair on it.

"Once more I'll ask. *Who scratched the decal?*"

The Indian Lady grabbed a stolen smorgasbord sugar packet from the table and stuffed it into her shoe. Now her legs were really gapped, angled for my grandfather's T-square.

I pointed at her shoe and my grandmother tried glancing over her shoulder—then stiffened as if she'd been pricked by a pin left in her homemade dress. "*She* scratched it? Don't test me, little liar." She grabbed her neck with her free hand. "Christ my artritis." She rubbed her neck and pushed the soap against my mouth.

I felt hair on my lips. I closed them tight against my teeth.

"Yes or no: Did—you—scratch—dat—DECAL."

I'd tasted Dial soap once before. My grandfather had been on strike. We'd run out of toothpaste and baking soda. "Darn management," my grandmother had said.

I looked cross-eyed at the Dial. So a kid scratches a decal? I thought, and those giant eyes sparkled at the corners. I nodded.

She eased off with the Dial. "You wanted to see under her towel, inna?"

I shook my head a little one.

"You wanted to see her *bozas*."

"*Bozas?*"

My grandmother gave me her longest, slowest shake of the head. "The desire is sinful," she said. "The sin of an adult. You'll burn like a chicken on the rotisserie. Now flush and go nap on the couch." She put the Dial back in the Shell Station ash tray, wiped her hands on the yellowed plastic of her apron, and walked back in the kitchen.

"Crazy," she said to the Indian Lady.

I closed the door. The little lady smiled. Decal, I thought, then flushed, went to the couch and took a nap.

When I woke, my grandfather was home from A.O. Smith. He made new car chasses there but was now sitting next to me cleaning the underside of his fingernails with a butterknife.

"Hello, Grandpa," I said.

He didn't say anything, just twitched.

"Did you make out on piecework today?"

He stood, slid the knife handle-first in his pocket, walked to the kitchen.

I watched him disappear, then stood and walked to the kitchen myself. My grandmother was there: on the wall phone, where people talked, unlike my grandfather, to her. My grand-father was sitting at the kitchen table behind his *Milwaukee Sentinel*, legs crossed like a pretzel knot. The knife lay on the table, pointed at my grandmother.

I sat down, eased the knife across the table and held it up to the pink light bulb hanging from the ceiling.

"Now he's threatening *Boze* at knifepoint," my grandmother told whoever was on the phone.

There was blue on the tip: decal remains. I stood to show them to my grandmother. Her shiny hand grabbed the knife tip. My hand was empty. She stepped to the sink. Eyebrows of purple cabbage floated in orange *kapusta* grease on the gray water. Whoever was on the phone was talking to her more than my grandfather would in a year. She dropped the knife. It sank.

The Steaks

A few weeks after my grandfather scratched the towel off the little lady, my grandmother and the Indian Lady began giving each other monthly Toni permanents. On these days—they were always Tuesdays—my grandparents' house smelled so much like women I'd have to go outside and do something, like catch flies the color of green Christmas ornaments and keep them in a used pickle jar with label glue still on it.

What I learned from this is that Christmas ornament green flies like to land in sunshine. And that if you put grass in a jar in sunshine to make a fly feel at home, either the fly will escape while you're opening the jar, or the next Tuesday the jar will sweat and the grass will stink yellow, with the fly lying on its back with its legs tangled like two stitches on your chin.

One Toni permanent day I was catching flies on the sunny side of the house. I couldn't smell women but I could still hear them talking through an open kitchen window.

The Indian Lady said she knew a woman with a daughter who neighbor ladies believed would sing like Judy Garland someday.

This was supposing Judy Garland would live.

The woman's name was Joan Hike and her husband's name was Norb Hike. Norb Hike had a worm farm and another daughter, older than the singing one, named Gertie Hike.

Then came the hushed stuff:

"That Gertie of hers stays out all night," the Indian Lady said. "Comes home at seven in the morning. Beer on the breath."

The next Saturday the Hikes invited us to their blocks-away house, a bankrupt corner hardware store with boarded-over windows. They invited us there to eat steak dinners and watch *The Virginian* on color TV.

I'd never done either.

When we opened their front door a little bell rang, just like it would in a hardware store.

My grandfather twitched.

The inside of the house looked like the inside of a hardware store without hardware in it: a giant room with shelves on the walls and a little back room you barely noticed.

The Indian Lady and two other people were in the big room sitting at a table, which was really a wooden door without doorknobs laid over two carpenter's horses.

"Joan and Norb Hike," the Indian Lady said.

"Sophie and Stanley," my grandmother said.

"Hi."

"Hello."

"How do, Stan."

My grandfather twitched.

Rust-colored freckles covered Joan Hike's skin, even her lips. We sat down. A fat older girl with several shades of yellow hair walked out of the little room, didn't say anything, and headed straight for the front door. The little bell rang and the door slammed. The Indian Lady looked at my grandmother, rolled her eyes. My grandmother nodded.

"That was our Gertie," Joan Hike said.

"Such beautiful hair," my grandmother said.

I didn't understand all this until years later, when I saw a woman with several shades of yellow hair on the cover of *Easyrider.*

Then a girl with a face white and smooth as Ivory soap walked in from the back room. Her hair was cut like a boy's and was brown, only one shade. She was about my age, which was five years old. She was Joan Hike's singing daughter, Pam Hike.

When everyone got quiet she sang "Somewhere Over the Rainbow" three times. She sang loud, with her eyes fluttering and her hands clasped over the space where her legs met.

When she finished, everyone clapped.

My grandmother clapped, nodded, and smiled.

"Like a professional," the Indian Lady said.

Norb Hike stood, finished clapping, and walked into the little room. He belched quietly in there, then yelled "SOUP'S ON."

My grandfather twitched. I knew what he was thinking: Soup we can eat at home for eight cents.

Norb Hike returned holding a foil-covered tray as if it were a litter of expensive poodles. He stood at the head of his homemade table and yanked away the foil. The tray said "PABST BLUE RIBBON" beneath burned meat pieces the size of Pam Hike's hands.

"Don't throw out dat foil," my grandmother said. "A man we know at the Seven Mile Fair buys it used."

Joan Hike looked at Norb Hike.

"How much," Norb Hike said.

"Two cents," my grandmother said.

Joan Hike raised her eyebrows.

"For five of those," my grandmother said.

Norb Hike scratched his armpit. "I need this one for Joan's incubator. You know all you need to hatch white meat is a box, ten square foot of this-here and a used sixty-watt."

"Maybe I can get him to give you three cents," my grandmother said.

Everyone stared at the foil, as if it were there to receive prayers. All I could hear was a miniature hacksaw: the Indian Lady trying to get enough air down her throat to supply her whole body.

Norb Hike pinched the blackest piece of meat, flipped it onto my dessert-sized plate.

"Salisbury," he told me.

I was excited about my first steak ever: rubbery hamburger you couldn't cut with a fork.

Actually it was a third of a steak. Pam Hike ate the second third. It was her first steak ever also, according to Joan Hike.

Norb Hike ate the third and biggest third, in addition to his whole steak.

I watched him eat the biggest third of my steak. He had a balding round head and smelled like a Firestone tire store. He sliced the third so hard it bled red juice all over his paper plate. He chewed, talking at my grandfather about his worm farm and things my grandmother and her lady friends never mentioned.

"What marks a true man," he said after he swallowed his last bite, "is a nose for a good used car."

My grandfather twitched. My grandmother looked at the Indian Lady. The Indian Lady looked at Joan Hike. Joan Hike looked at Norb Hike, put her finger over her lips, shook her head.

"Not around the little one," she whispered, and no one—
not even Pam Hike—looked at me.

"Why not?" Norb Hike said.

"Used cars," my grandmother whispered.

I looked at Norb Hike's steak blood, then Pam Hike.

Used cars, I thought. Why not?

The Fair

My grandparents were 3Ps.

3P means Poor Polish Person.

My grandparents lived in 3P territory, the South Side of Milwaukee.

Every Sunday they'd take me to the Seven Mile Fair in my grandfather's brand new Oldsmobile. I never wanted to go but they'd take me anyway.

The Seven Mile Fair was an outdoor flea market seven miles south of Milwaukee. My grandfather had a twenty-year lease on a shack there. He stored used things in the shack and tried to sell them to other 3Ps on Sundays. He sold used buttons, used thread, used yarn and used pins and needles. He sold used ribbon and used wrapping paper and used statues of saints and used barstools and used calendars with pictures of shiny ladies wearing high heels and bathing suits. He tried to sell a very used brass clock that I wasn't supposed to touch and no one could afford.

"Why can't I touch it?" I'd ask him.

He'd look away.

"It's an *antique*," my grandmother would say.

He made a lot of his money off 3Ps' kids. He sold them hard, dusty bubblegum he bought by the gross at auctions, used water pistols that leaked, and used cap guns without caps.

The only new things he sold were balloons and sparklers.

I had to blow up the balloons and stand there holding them. "Balloons," I had to say. "Balloons."

"You don't say it loud enough," my grandfather would tell me, using two-thirds of his daily word average.

"Balloons," I'd say.

"How much?" a kid walking past the shack might say.

"A nickel," I was supposed to say. "A dime for helium. These dandy Mickey Mouse ones with the ears are a quarter."

Then I was supposed to put the used string tied to a Mickey Mouse one in the kid's hand and ask the kid's young-looking grandfather for a quarter.

The Sunday after my first third-of-a-steak dinner I stood in front of my grandfather's Seven Mile Fair shack holding balloons for four and a half hours.

I stood in the direct sun and said "balloons" 756 times.

I didn't sell a single balloon.

When the sun started setting, a Mickey Mouse balloon popped without me moving or taking a used pin or anything to it.

My grandfather twitched.

"There goes twenty-five cents," my grandmother said.

Sometimes she'd interpret like that.

What I learned from this is that the sun pops balloons. My grandfather didn't believe that, but my grandmother did:

"Why sure it was the sun. What else?"

My grandfather twitched.

"Come on, Stanley. Here. Take a quarter from my profits. That Mexeecan woman bought my used grocery bags. Take it. It's not your profits, *Stashu*. It's mine. Take it so you two are even. Or I'll give to the little one. *Take* it."

My grandfather took it.

My grandfather made most of *his* profits selling sparklers. Sparklers were illegal in Wisconsin but my grandfather knew a man in Illinois who wholesaled factory seconds for next to nothing. You had to be part of the bad-kid underworld to know my grandfather sold them because he hid them deep in his shack, behind his leaky helium tank and stacked carpet samples. It got very hot back there that Sunday in June, with sparklers stocked deep for the Fourth of July and my cigar-smoking grandfather filling helium balloons that popped for strange reasons.

The Sausage

My grandfather's brand new Oldsmobile had power windows.

The first time I touched a power window button, the sudden power window noise made my grandfather twitch.

"Don't touch dat," my grandmother told me. She was sitting next to me in the back seat wearing her newest used dress. This was nine days after the balloon popped.

Norb Hike was in the front seat with my grandfather. They smoked cigars the color of pea soup, their blue smoke twisting in the oncoming sunshine like slow motion snakes. The green speedometer needle moved and pointed: 75.

We were late for bingo. My grandmother kept looking at her pocket watch, which she'd bought used from another man's shack at the Seven Mile Fair and kept hidden in her purse. The blinking Allen Bradley tower said it was hot for Milwaukee: 84. Allen Bradley was a factory. Everyone except my grandfather worked there.

We got to St. Josaphat's Hall at twelve after seven. St. Josaphat's was our parish. Usually we got there at six-thirty. Joan Hike was in St. Luke's Hospital getting kidney stones removed. The Indian Lady was at a button factory closeout. Bingo wasn't everything.

My grandfather turned off the ignition and Norb Hike pointed to a dial on the dashboard. "She's runnin' awful hot, Stanley."

Everyone got quiet, as if we were going to church. But it was Saturday. Church was closed. We went to the hall.

There weren't four seats together so I had to sit apart from my grandparents, next to a fat woman in a hairnet. Most women there had one or two fat body parts, but this was one of those XL fatties who wore dresses cut from bedsheets and hula-hoops for belts. The only normal-sized thing on her was that hairnet.

She played nine bingo cards at a time, kissed a plastic statue of St. Francis before every call, and had six inches of arm flab. Two calls after I sat there she stood, yelled "whole card" and was brought fifteen pounds of *kielbasa*.

Then she let out a small fart.

Two bingos later the police came and unplugged the bingo caller's microphone and told everyone to leave.

We were violating state law, they said.

They took three dozen eggs from a bald man without shoulders.

Mrs. Hairnet gave me her *kielbasa*, pointed to a darkened doorway next to the stage, and told me she'd give me a nickel if I'd meet her in the parking lot with all fifteen pounds.

I watched her arm flab jiggle while I thought it over. Then I took the *kielbasa*, walked through the doorway and fell straight down a flight of stairs. I held onto the *kielbasa* as if I were a Green Bay Packer. After I stopped falling I sat in the dark for a long time tasting blood in the back of my throat.

Then a light went on. A policeman stood at the top of the stairs. "Where you going?" he said.

"The parking lot. I think I have a nosebleed."

"Put your head back."

I put my head back and he led me to the parking lot by the nose. I still had the *kielbasa*. Two cars sat near the convent, a rusty red one and my grandfather's brand new Oldsmobile. Mrs. Hairnet was sitting in the red one acting like she wasn't there— no easy task for a woman her size. The policeman looked at her, pointed at the *kielbasa*, raised his eyebrows. She started the car and took off.

My grandparents and Norb Hike were standing around my grandfather's new car, looking at a green puddle between the front tires.

"She overheated," Norb Hike said. "Brand new and she overheated."

"This your kid?" the policeman said.

Everyone got quiet.

"Sir?" Norb Hike said.

"This your kid?"

"Yes, officer," Norb Hike said. "Helped me deliver them sausages to the hall this evening." He nodded at the *kielbasa*. "My donation to the parish."

The policeman took the *kielbasa* and gave it to Norb Hike.

"Start keeping an eye out for this kid." He glanced at the green puddle, then glared at my grandfather for a long time.

"And *you*," he said to my grandfather. "You keep your sausage to yourself."

My grandfather twitched.

The policeman glared for another three seconds, then left.

"What does he mean, *sau*sage?" my grandmother said. "I didn't know you had sausage, Stanley. Did you buy wholesale to sell at the Fair? What does he mean *sau*sage?"

Norb Hike and I looked at each other.

"*Sau*sage," my grandmother said.

The Kiss

All the houses on my grandparents' block looked the same. Some were different colors, but they all looked the same. They were bungalows.

Most of them had siding that looked like roof shingles—with tiny stones on them and tar underneath—but all of them had painted-gray wooden porches.

Whoever sold that paint was a millionaire.

My grandparents' porch had a hollow beneath it. There were gray trellises around the hollow so you might not think it was there, but it was there.

All the trellises were nailed to the porch except one. I learned this the morning my grandfather prepared to fix a rain gutter. He took off the loose trellis, crawled under the porch to get a ladder, then moved things around in there without saying anything for a long time.

I wanted to take his claw hammer and common nails and cage him in there. But I didn't do that.

My grandfather was already a nervous man.

There was one building on my grandparents' block that didn't have a gray porch or shingled siding: the firehouse. The firehouse was all red bricks and no porch. It was on the corner and the firetruck always had its red nose poked into the driveway, sniffing out smoke.

The firemen sat in varnished chairs leaned against the red brick, their hair combed like hairpieces. Neighbor ladies walked past them and nodded. They were American heroes.

Across the street from the firehouse was Helen Pickadilly's house. She was another lady friend of my grandmother. Her house was a bankrupt sweet shop. According to my grandmother, at one time everyone in the neighborhood liked Helen Pickadilly because she sold sweets. But not anymore: she'd sold her sweets too cheap.

She didn't live in her bankrupt sweet shop like the Hikes lived in their bankrupt corner hardware store. She lived in the back room only.

I never got to go in the back room, though. The only time I was near it was the Saturday after my nosebleed. And my grandmother didn't take me there. My grandfather did. My grandmother was shopping with her coupons and the Indian Lady.

When my grandfather and I got to Helen Pickadilly's, he didn't knock, just opened the front door and walked in as if he had a savings account there. I followed. The windows were covered with swirls of white liquid shoe polish, but the silver malt machines and glittery red swivel chairs still sparkled.

My grandfather made me sit on a swivel chair and not swivel. As if a kid could swivel his way to Red China.

Then he walked behind the counter and knocked on a varnished wooden door.

A woman in a white robe walked out, Helen Pickadilly. She was skinny and wore perfume that smelled like gardenias but above all was very pale and wore a lot of rouge.

She ruffled my hair, pinched my cheek, looked me in the eye and said I was going to a be a big, handsome man someday.

My grandfather spoke Polish, passing his nine-word-a-day average in two seconds. She answered in Polish. He answered back. The veins in his neck looked hard. They had a ping pong conversation, like human beings, but in Polish.

I wondered if they were discussing something the police weren't supposed to know about, like sausage.

When it was time to leave, Helen Pickadilly asked me for a kiss. I looked at my grandfather—who twitched—and my face turned silent and hot as a burner on a stove.

Helen Pickadilly's orange lips curved up like a melon rind, showing her yellow teeth. I'd never seen lips do that before. Whatever they were doing looked painful. Then they got closer, kissed my cheek, and left it wet.

My grandfather and I walked out the front door. Helen Pickadilly stood in the shaded doorway in her robe, lips curved up, squinting and waving with orange lipstick on her teeth. Her face was the color of waxed paper. Mine was red. I could smell her saliva drying on my cheek. My grandfather smelled like gardenias.

The firetruck got a good whiff of everything.

My grandfather and I walked along the shady side of the sweet shop, then headed down the cobblestone alley for home. I held my grandfather's thumb, which felt like a dill pickle with a heart beat.

An empty police car sat beside Helen Pickadilly's garage. I wanted to ask what the policeman at bingo had meant about sausage, but decided that wasn't a kid's business. I pointed at the police car, which had a dent in one door.

"Is that a good used car, Grandpa?" I asked.

The dill pickle twitched from my fist like a cork from a liniment bottle.

"Does that mean yes?" I asked, and my grandfather had his worst-ever twitch fit, coughing, shrugging, hissing breath in and out through his nose.

When the fit ended, he walked faster than I could, as if I were the sausage policeman myself.

The Sleeping Larry Show

The Tuesday after I saw inside the front of Helen Pickadilly's sweet shop, my grandmother and the Indian Lady talked about taxes:

"That darn state butter tax is the worst."

"Three cents extra a pound, I heard."

"Ridiculous."

Then they came up with a plan: drive to Waukegan, Illinois, buy 700 sticks of tax-free butter, and sell them at the Seven Mile Fair at a profit.

At dinner that night, my grandmother asked my grandfather to drive to Waukegan.

My grandfather didn't say anything, just read his paper and ate *kielbasa* my grandmother had bought cheap from Joan Hike.

The next morning my grandmother and I walked four blocks to Anna's bungalow, which was smaller than my grandparents' house but had more junk.

Anna was the oldest of my grandmother's lady friends. She kept a talking parakeet named Ricky in a wire cage in her kitchen. She'd gotten Ricky half-price at Kresge's because its beak was chipped. She'd spent weeks teaching Ricky to talk, sitting by the cage and saying words 100 times so Ricky could watch her lips move. When Ricky learned a new word, she'd let him out of his cage.

Ricky knew fourteen words, all Polish.

When my grandmother and I got to Anna's house that morning, Ricky was flying all over the kitchen. He'd just learned the word *tsa.*

Tsa means "what."

Anna dug through a shoebox full of cookie crumbs, found a worn piece of cookie, put it next to her toaster oven, and said, "Here."

Ricky kept flying.

"*Eat.*"

Ricky kept flying.

My grandmother snapped her fingers in front of my face. "In a daze, he is."

Anna put the piece of cookie against my lips. It smelled a little like coconut but a lot like her house. I let it in.

My grandmother sat at the kitchen table and explained her butter-smuggling plan. When she and Anna began speaking Polish, Ricky understood more than I did.

I walked out of the kitchen and into the living room, to spit out the cookie. Larry, Anna's husband, sat on his Lay-Z-Boy, watching television in his sleep.

Larry was even older than Anna. His pink head was round but the white hairs standing on top of it were flat as a mowed lawn. His stomach filled his pants like a beach ball and his feet weren't touching the floor. His nose whistled, and the cigar in his mouth had an ash two inches long.

My grandfather's ashes never grew half that length.

The television program was ladies talking. Christ, I thought. Everywhere I go. I swallowed the cookie, sat on the floor, and watched Larry's ash grow a quarter-inch.

Then his dentures began sliding from his mouth, clamped on the wet end of the cigar. I scooted closer. I liked being one of the boys.

Then I heard flapping: Ricky had flown into the room. He landed on Larry's head, chirped Polish I didn't understand, and hopped on Larry's cigar. The ash fell, rolled over Larry's leather-coin shirt buttons, landed somewhere beneath the beach ball. Smoke rose from between his legs and one of his eyes opened.

I crawled behind the Lay-Z-Boy so he wouldn't see me. I didn't want to embarrass him: there was a parakeet on his cigar.

His nose whistled a few times and then I heard my darned grandmother:

"What you doing behind that Lay-Z-Boy?"

"*Tsa?*" Ricky said.

"You heard me."

Ricky cocked his head toward the ceiling and I noticed my grandmother wasn't looking at him. She was looking at *me*.

"Kneeling," I said.

"Kneeling on electricity, hey. Extension cords, those are.

And tangled yet. Are you crazy? Get out here."

I got out there.

My grandmother touched Larry's wrist. "Is my little one bothering you?"

Larry's nose whistled. Ricky cocked his head and chirped.

"The goshdarned parrot-keet," my grandmother said, and Ricky took off, fluttering headfirst into a blue sky on the television.

"Our little one is hungry?" a voice said: Anna was waddling into the room with a rag over her shoulder.

I couldn't think of an answer. Ricky chirped Polish and Anna shooed him toward the kitchen with the rag. "Then get," she said, "your ess back to your cage."

My grandmother stood watching the television. "A true picture," she said.

"And used, we bought it. Used ones play good."

The television screen flashed, then went black.

"*Oh* Lord," my grandmother said. Anna knelt and my grandmother covered her glasses with her forearm. "It won't explode, no?"

I stepped toward the kitchen and something tugged at my ankle. I looked down: an extension cord. Anna began changing channels. The dial was noisy. My grandmother closed her eyes and Larry's nose whistled—out, in, out. I crawled behind the Lay-Z-Boy, put the brown plug in the socket. The TV went on: more ladies talking. Do they ever stop? I thought, and I crawled to my grandmother's leg, which was covered with skin the color of warm liverwurst.

"There," my grandmother said.

"Huh?"

"Picture's back."

"I'll be darned."

Larry's nose stopped whistling, his eyes open a sixteenth of an inch.

"And your husband's awake."

Anna grunted, took Larry's cigar, adjusted his dentures. He licked his lips and she asked him to drive her, my grandmother and the Indian Lady to Waukegan. His eyes ricocheted from side to side and she held his cigar an inch beyond his outstretched tongue. Then we heard his voice, which sounded distant, as if his face were a radio.

"Sure," his voice said.

Her Electrical

When I was five I slept in my grandmother's sewing room. It was actually a closet but also her sewing room and my bedroom, too. I slept on a burlap sack of pillow stuffing surrounded by bolts of material, stacked dress pattern envelopes, a Singer sewing machine, and a mannequin. If the Russians invaded the United States of America, I was probably safe.

But the Russians never did that.

The mannequin wasn't like the ones my grandfather kept on the rafters in the garage. This mannequin had clothes on.

The morning of the Butter Run I woke to the noise of my grandfather rinsing his face. I say noise for a reason:

When my grandfather rinsed his face he'd cup his hands and fill them with water, then splash his face and twitch air from his nose, spraying water like a sparrow wearing an elephant's trunk in a birdbath.

Breakfast was cinammon toast. My grandfather folded his first piece, crammed it into his mouth, and *said* something:

"No sugar mixed in?"

"We're running low," my grandmother said. She pointed at me with a knife shiny from old butter. "The little one must be snitching again."

I swallowed my first bite. "The Indian Lady—"

"Shush."

I shushed and finished my one slice.

My grandfather finished four slices, got up and left for work with his mouth closed: only five words left for the day. My grandmother and I did dishes, then took a bath in the same water. After she washed and rinsed herself everywhere, she reached under the water. "Let's washrag your shoo-shoo."

Again? I thought, and I looked away, at the clothes chute.

The little lady was watching me, her towel scratched completely away.

"What you looking at?" my grandmother said.

"*Oops!*" the little lady said with her Life Saver smile.

My grandmother's hand found the place where my legs met. She squeezed. "Grandma's *talking*, little one."

And I'm listening, I thought.

"Grandma's asking at what you were looking."

I squeezed the sides of her fist with my thighs. "Grandpa's decal."

Her fingernails dug in. "Whose decal?"

"Grandpa's."

"For God's *sake*," she said, and she let go. "Rinse off and get dressed for our car trip."

I did that. Then I got as far away from her as I could, pressing myself against the living room window until Larry's green-blue car pulled up to our curb, with Larry, Anna, and the Indian Lady inside. The horn beeped and my grandmother grabbed my arm and pulled me out of the house. As we walked down the gray porch stairs, the car engine screamed. Larry, hands on the steering wheel and the beach ball in his pants, was smiling.

My grandmother and I got in the car.

"New, this is?" my grandmother said.

Anna shook her head. "Used. But a Ford. A forty-nine Ford Tudor."

"Right after the war," Larry said.

I had to sit in the back seat with the Indian Lady. She didn't look at me, and I felt invisible all the way to Waukegan.

In Waukegan we bought 700 sticks of butter from a man on a warehouse loading dock. The sticks weren't in boxes and some had smashed corners, but they were a penny a stick cheaper that way.

We packed four ten-pound ice blocks and 674 sticks of butter in Larry's trunk.

"That's damn good payload," the loading dock man said.

On the trip back, the twenty-six extra sticks of butter sat in a used plastic bag between me and the Indian Lady. The ones on the her side of the bag began melting at the Wisconsin-Illinois border.

Ten miles later, a Wisconsin State Trooper pulled Larry over.

"Know how fast you were going, old timer?"

Anna reached under the front seat, pulled out a phone book, and leaned across Larry's beach ball. "Half-speed," she said. "We keep this under the pedal."

"1O3 miles an hour," the Trooper said.

Larry looked at me out of the corner of his eye and smirked.

The Trooper searched the glove compartment. Sweat striped the back of Anna's neck while he wrote the ticket.

We got to Milwaukee. Larry opened his trunk. The butter was soft but still in sticks. Larry drove us to the butcher shop. The butcher let us store the butter in his cooler in exchange for the ten sticks that hadn't melted in the plastic bag between me and the Indian Lady.

Larry drove us to my grandmother's house. He sat at the kitchen table and smoked with his eyes closed while my grandmother, Anna, and the Indian Lady "diveed" the melted butter in the plastic bag. My grandmother and the Indian Lady got two cups each. Anna got three and a half cups.

Anna got the extra cup and a half because Larry drove.

The Indian Lady said, "Supper time." Anna grabbed Larry's cigar and his eyes opened. Then everyone left.

My grandmother used her melted butter to make a pound cake. She also made chicken soup from frozen neck bones left over from seventy-eight days before.

The pound cake rose, didn't fall, turned brown. The wall clock said a minute past six. "No Grandpa," my grandmother said, and she and I ate half of the chicken soup.

Then we sat watching the clock hands.

"Quarter after and no Grandpa," my grandmother eventually said, and we ate half of the *diluted* chicken soup.

Finally she began slicing the pound cake. "Thirty past and no Grandpa," she said, and keys jingled behind the back door. My grandfather walked in—with Norb Hike behind him:

"It's her electrical, Stanley. In the wiring, I mean. First she overheats and now her electrical is shot. A new radiator I can see but the last thing you wanna mess with is her electrical. Replace your battery, alternator, generator, regulator, coil, cap, condenser, points and plug wires and she still might not start. Or she'll start today and lay dead on you before church one morning."

My grandfather stared at Norb Hike's lips as if Norb Hike were teaching him English.

"Or before work."

My grandfather twitched.

Norb Hike sliced himself an inch-thick piece of pound cake,

bit half of it off, held the rest in front of his mouth.

"Plus your payments?" he said. Crumbs fell from his mouth like white specks from the empty laundry detergent boxes my grandmother would hold upside down and slap to save money. "I say sell her, Stanley. Sell her and buy a good used one. Darn new cars never did anyone any good."

My grandmother glared at my grandfather.

 **Liquid**

St. Josaphat's had an Irish pastor, Father Pat. A week after my grandfather started having electrical problems, Father Pat's sister got married at St. Josaphat's, with Father Pat doing the ceremony. You could say Father Pat married his sister, but then again you might not want to say that.

Father Pat's sister was forty-three years old, with jagged teeth like a shark's. Hardly any men liked her but a cobbler with hair in his ears did and she married him.

My grandmother sewed the wedding dress, which meant I slept beside it weeks before the cobbler did.

Father Pat's sister's reception was in a rented hall beneath a bowling alley. The hall had a low ceiling and an accordian band. Between songs I'd hear bowling balls roll the length of the ceiling and pins crack like thunder over the wedding cake.

I was standing next to my grandmother and the Indian Lady with a Pepsi-Cola in my hand when Father Pat's sister tossed her bouquet.

Gertie Hike caught it.

The Indian Lady looked at my grandmother and rolled her eyes.

"For God's *sake*," my grandmother said.

Then the accordion band played "I Wish I Was Single Again."

"I Wish I Was Single Again" went like this:

> I wish I was single again.
> I wish I was single again.
> 'Cause if I was single
> My pockets would jingle.
> I wish I was single again.

People actually polkaed to that song. While they did, I went upstairs to watch bowlers. Most of them were men who wore slicked-back hair and smelled like clothes hampers. One of them was Norb Hike.

I sat watching him from a gray formica table with pictures of big red dice on it. He had on black tuxedo pants and an untucked tanktop T-shirt. He was holding his hands over the tiny fan on the bowling ball rack when he saw me. "Smile," he said.

I'd never heard the word before.

He pointed to his lips, which curved up, showing his square yellow teeth. This "smile" isn't something Polish, I thought—because I'd never seen one on my grandparents. He put a cigar in his, grabbed a pearly brown ball, and squatted, the crack of his behind winking over his cummerbund like a peach over a grocery bag.

Then he bowled. His brown ball hit every pin, sent three spinning back up the alley. He nodded, walked back to make sure his partner put the "X" down. He saw me, stepped toward my table and smiled.

"Why aren't you downstairs cuttin' the rug?"

You had to watch the cigar bounce to understand him.

"I don't dance," I said, "if I don't have to."

His cigar sprang stiff against his pig nose. "Don't dance if you don't have to? Is that what you said?" He elbowed his partner, nodded at an orange-haired woman working the bar, and smiled. His cigar had good posture. "Kid says he don't dance if he don't have to."

His partner smiled, squinted at the woman's orange hair.

Norb Hike elbowed him harder. "You gotta like a kid like that, hey Liquid?"

"Sure," Liquid said. He bit the head off a celery stalk in the red drink in his hand. "Who's a smart kid like that belong to?"

"Neighbor buddy of mine Stanley," Norb Hike said. "Kid's his grandson."

Liquid stood, stared at me, and then bowled. He had a bulldog tattoo on his forearm and a black ball that clipped pins like a lawnmower. He walked back and made sure Norb Hike put the "X" down. He looked at me, ate celery, and didn't smile. "This buddy of yours Stanley need wheels?" he asked Norb Hike.

Norb Hike turned his head so I wouldn't hear, but I heard:

"Sure does, Johnny," he said, cigar nodding. "Though he don't quite know it yet."

Johnny? I thought. Is he Liquid or Johnny?

"Like maybe he'll lose his lid?" the man said. He stepped over to the redhead, who poured him a drink.

Liquid Johnny? I thought.

Norb Hike's cigar nodded.

The Hitch

The day after Father Pat's sister got married was the day my grandmother and the Indian Lady hoped to sell 674 sticks of butter at a profit.

That morning the Indian Lady walked my grandmother, my grandfather and me to Anna's house. In Anna's kitchen, a Red Owl grocery bag covered Ricky's cage.

"My Ricky is napping," Anna told me. She sat on the kitchen table and grunted as she snapped garters onto her stockings. "I finish and we go," she told my grandfather between grunts.

I preferred not to watch. I went in the living room. Larry was there, on his Lay-Z-Boy. With his closed eyes, hanging feet, and cigar ash, he was a picture of his old self. The only thing missing was his nose-whistling.

I put my ear next to his nose to make sure. Then I knelt in front of him and watched his ash grow an inch and his pink head turn gray.

"Up, sleepy one," a voice said: Anna was waddling into the room.

I stood and she pushed me aside. She asked Larry seventeen questions, then told him he was a lazy, good-as-gone man.

Then came the screaming and crying.

We never did go to the Seven Mile Fair that Sunday. The Indian Lady wanted to but there were other things to do.

If that Sunday were a box of 674 sticks of butter and Larry's silent body, its directions would have been simple:

Store in a cool, dry place.

# Rags

My grandparents did not have much lawn. There was barely room for skinny shaded sidewalks between the houses on their block, so they had no side lawns, just front and back ones.

Their front lawn was forty-two feet long but all hill, so not a lot of running room between the porch and traffic.

I say running room because there was no walking down that hill without running.

That left the back lawn, seventy-nine square feet of grass between the house and the garage. The only thing a kid could do there was dig through crabgrass roots for those little brown balls of insect armor that didn't look alive, and try to trick them into moving.

The day Larry went six feet under I spent the early morning sitting on the back lawn. I got mad at six brown balls of insect armor, then tried something new: closing one eye at a time.

When I closed one eye at a time, my grandparents' house moved, making the yard look longer. But it only moved back and forth. It never cleared the lot.

I had one eye closed when I heard a faint voice from the alley, a man's voice saying the same word over and over. I couldn't make out the word but the echo sounded Polish.

I ran behind the ashcan and spied up the alley, a red cobble-stone hill in front of the voice. For awhile nothing happened, but then a hat appeared over the cobblestones, on an old man's head on an old man's body pulling what looked like a wagon. The man's cheeks looked like he was sucking a cherry malted through a straw but his mouth was empty, opening into a black dot a moment before I'd hear the sound of that lonely word.

That far away, he was scaring piss drops out of me.

Splotches of white flew from the garages on either side him onto the back of the wagon. One splotch hit his shoulder but landed in the pile behind him.

When he was three garages away I still couldn't understand what he was saying but looked at the pile and figured it out myself.

"Rags," I whispered. He passed me and nodded. His wagon was actually the back half of an old used car, with the trunk open and pipes duct-taped to its gray sides for handles. Cobblestone made its wheels wobble.

I nodded back.

Two hours later Larry went six feet under, in St. Stanislaus Cemetery.

But before he did, he went on display at The Bruno A. Pruski Funeral Parlor.

My grandparents and I got to the parlor late because my grandfather splashed my grandmother while washing his face, and she had to change dresses. When we got there everyone was kneeling, except Larry.

"Ugh," my grandmother said as we knelt.

Father Pat stood in front of Larry and talked, touching his fingertips together and opening them like blooming tulips. When he sat on a padded folding chair everyone stood and got in a line moving toward Larry.

The person at the front of the line had to take a holy water sprinkler from the person who'd just been in front of him, look at Larry, shake the sprinkler at his head, and walk back to the unpadded folding chairs with straight lips.

I got to the front of the line. My grandmother gave me the sprinkler. It looked like a brass microphone without a cord. I had the urge to tap it and blow into it and say "O-69," like a bingo caller.

But I didn't do that. Instead I shook it three times. Nothing came out. A nice feeling pressed out from inside me, tried to leave through my lips. I didn't let it. I kept my lips straight like everyone else, pushing the nice feeling back inside.

Larry lay there without a drop on him. I wondered if he felt something nice inside also. If he did, his straight lips held it back easily—thanks to body work done by Bruno A. Pruski.

Green Rain

Three days after Larry went six feet under was a Sunday. I woke up that morning to the sound of my grandfather washing his face, saw my grandmother's mannequin and thought:

Seven Mile Fair Day.

Christ.

We went to church without eating breakfast, which meant we had something important to sell at the Fair. St. Josaphat's church was a *basilica*: a high ceiling that was shaped like a bubble and wasn't held up by anything.

I knew what happened to bubbles and didn't like kneeling under a heavy one. So after Father Pat opened the gold safe behind the altar, I pulled my grandmother's sleeve and pointed up. "What keeps it from falling?" I asked.

"*Boze*," she said. "Now give to the usher." She pressed a smooth dime, the kind with the devil-lady on it, onto my palm.

An old man wearing a tie put a basket in my hand. It was lined with green felt and contained crumpled dollars. The man had a solid brown bubble the size of a pencil eraser attached to the corner of his eye. He nodded. I dropped the dime. Maybe the money would keep his bubble from popping also.

Father Pat began in on the Latin. My grandmother lent me her spare rosary and I prayed, asking God to make the Russians bomb the Seven Mile Fair.

The ceiling never fell but when we got home the The Indian Lady was sitting on the porch. Her legs weren't apart: Sunday. We took her with us to the butcher, put the butter and ice in the trunk of my grandfather's brand new Oldsmobile, and started for the Seven Mile Fair.

I had to sit in front with my grandfather. There weren't any air raid sirens and I watched telephone wires on the other side of Highway 41 go up and down like waves.

Then a thump struck the roof of the car. I looked at my grandfather. He was looking out the back window as if his chin were connected to his shoulder, driving eighty-four miles an hour.

My grandmother and the Indian Lady had their chins connected to their shoulders also: behind us, my grandfather's hood was turning cartwheels on Highway 41, back toward Milwaukee. It tightroped the dotted yellow line for a few spins and fell flat in front of a car with a checkerboard grill.

The car handled that hood like a tank over newspaper.

My grandfather twitched.

"Oy yoy," my grandmother said.

I turned and looked out the windshield. My grandfather's brand new Oldsmobile was crossing the yellow line, speeding eighty-nine miles an hour at a silver eagle on an oncoming car.

"Grandpa," I said.

The eagle's wings grew wider.

"Grandpa."

My grandfather looked at me. I pointed. My grandfather cranked the steering wheel a good one—and the car missed us.

"For God's *sake*," my grandmother said.

My grandfather pulled onto the emergency lane, did a U-turn, headed back toward his hood.

"The butter," the Indian Lady said.

My grandfather accelerated for a few seconds, then hit the brake. We spun like a card but didn't flip over: dealt clean. We were off the highway in tall green grass.

There was a huddle of black and white cows nearby, grazing. They lifted their eyes our way but their heads stayed still and their mouths kept chewing.

My grandfather and I got out and walked to the hood. It was striped with tire tread. My grandfather ran his finger up and down the tread. The tread stayed there.

My grandfather made me grab an end of the hood. We walked it to his car like a stretcher to an ambulance. The cows stopped chewing to watch. When we got to the car my grandmother gave my grandfather her longest, slowest shake of the head. "That butter," she said, and my grandfather dropped the hood on my fingers.

"Ow."

My grandfather stared at the hood as if it were a naked mannequin—or Helen Pickadilly waving goodbye in her robe.

"Fifty foot from these cows," he said. "Remember that."

Seven words, I thought. He's beginning to talk as much as a woman. I kept my lips straight and we got in the car. My grandfather turned the ignition key and the engine screamed. The temperature needle swept past "H," disappeared.

My grandfather twitched.

"The butter," my grandmother said.

This time the Indian Lady shook her head. "A high of eighty-five today, the blond weatherman predicted."

"And the humidity. Did he say the humidity?"

"He said the humidity."

My grandfather drove through the tall green grass as if there really was an air raid. His car, I imagined, was a jeep. My grandmother was the pilot and the Indian Lady was the bombardier:

"Hotter already it seems."

"Look at my perspiration. See my perspiration?"

"Through your hair it's running. I'll have to give you another permanent free."

"Through yours too it's running."

"I can feel it run. You feel yours run?"

"Why sure."

"That butter."

"Can you imagine?"

My fingers felt better: numb.

My grandfather turned onto Highway 41, put his foot to the floor. He was going ninety when drops began attaching themselves to the windshield. "What's this?" the Indian Lady said. "Rain on the windshield with no clouds in the sky? Did he say rain, the weatherman?"

My grandfather pulled the wiper button. The wipers stayed still. Drops kept attaching themselves.

"I can't see," my grandfather said. "Can you see?"

Six more words, I thought. Including a question. The man is out of control.

"Should he put the wiperwashers on?" the Indian Lady said.

"A license I don't have," my grandmother said. "But wiper-washers he should put on."

I tried to stick my head out my window but the window was up and my head bounced off it instead. My grandfather's head did the same thing. Then his finger touched his power window switch. Nothing happened—not even the sudden noise.

I tried my power window switch. My grandmother's mouth kept shut, but so did the window. My grandfather pulled over, got out, looked at the windshield from the outside. He ran his finger back and forth through the drops. They moved like quicksilver, but not off the windshield.

I got out, heard the sound of a teapot ready to whistle. The drops were light green, like diluted mouthwash.

"Antifreeze," my grandfather said: his longest English word ever.

"The hood would have kept it off the windshield," I said, and he switched back to good old twitching.

We don't have the hood, the twitches said. Those cows have the hood.

A car coming at us stopped on the other side of the highway. A man got out and came over. He wore a long-sleeve shirt and had gray hair: a long-sleeve shirt in eighty-six degree weather, and when he got closer his hair looked tinted—and tinted gray, not black.

Jesuz Kochani, I thought. What the heck kind of—

"Car trouble?" the man said. His eyes bounced off mine to my grandfather's. "Radiator?"

My grandfather nodded.

"No hood?" the man said. He began looking familiar, like a week-old leftover *pierogi*.

My grandfather shook his head. I pointed in the direction of the cows, but the man and my grandfather watched the radiator with their arms crossed like wooden Indians. The radiator hissed louder.

I walked across the highway and looked at the man's car. From behind it looked used, and Polish: a fat Polish face with straight lips and red eyes. I stepped in front of it, saw the checkerboard. The car that ran over the hood, I thought, and I glanced across the street at the man in the long sleeves and gray tint. Johnny, I thought. Liquid Johnny.

I ran back to my grandfather's car. My grandmother was sitting on the trunk, the man in the driver's seat. He turned the ignition key. *Nothing*: like the inside of St. Josaphat's the Sunday after my grandfather had forgotten to set the clocks ahead.

"It's your electrical," the man said. He turned the key again and I saw, through his shirtsleeve, the bulldog tattoo.

"Grandpa," I said.

My grandfather gazed at the sky.

"Grandpa." I tugged on his wallet pocket, a sure way to get his attention. "Grandpa."

"Damn electrical'll cost ya two arms and two legs," Liquid Johnny said.

My grandfather twitched.

Liquid Johnny didn't smile. "What year is she?"

"Nineteen fifty-nine," my grandmother said.

"Grandpa."

"Damn new cars never did anyone any good."

I pulled my grandfather's wallet from his pocket. Suddenly everyone was looking at me—except Liquid Johnny. I pointed at him. "He—"

"What's with this pocketpicketing?" my grandmother said. "Give Grandpa back or I'll spank your behind blue. In front of these cars going by."

I was still pointing at Liquid Johnny. "He bowled with Norb Hike at Father Pat's sister's wedding. They said—"

My grandfather grabbed his wallet.

I tried to tug it back. "They said you'd lose a lid and need a used—"

My grandmother whapped me a good one.

I let go of the wallet. "Car."

The Indian Lady spread her legs to get out of the back seat, her girdle the color of an old bandage. "Such an imagination," she said without looking at me. "Where does he get such an imagination?"

I felt invisible again.

"And the butter?" she said. "Like soup, I bet."

"The butter," my grandmother said to my grandfather. "What about the butter?"

My grandfather took the key from the ignition. We watched him open the trunk.

"*Jezus Kochani*," my grandmother said:

The trunk was a yellow Lake Michigan containing 674 butter stick wrappers and a spare tire.

The Indian Lady didn't say a thing. Her eyes did all the talking.

We stood looking at the butter for a long time, as if standing and looking might make it harden back into sticks.

But the butter never did that.

Instead it dripped like eggtimer sand from the right taillight to the emergency lane.

It dripped until Liquid Johnny and my grandfather drove off in the used car with the checkerboard grill, and kept dripping until they returned two hours later with a tow truck behind them.

The tow truck had words on its driver's side door:

HONEST JOHN'S WRECKER SERVICE

The tow truck driver's name was Stu. He had a clean-shaven face but inch-long neck hairs up to the dimple on his chin. I had to sit in the tow truck alongside him on the way back to Milwaukee. Ten empty Lucky Strike packs sat on his dashboard, nine of them crumpled.

When Liquid Johnny's used car reached the black and white cows, we pulled over. The cows were still grazing but were now scattered like outfielders in County Stadium.

I sat in the crowd of neck hairs and Lucky Strikes packs and watched my grandfather walk circles through tall green grass shading his eyes like a saluting soldier.

Liquid Johnny looked also, but without walking. He gave up before my grandfather did and got back in his used car.

When my grandfather stopped saluting, Stu scratched some neck hairs, took a cigarette from the uncrumpled pack, and lit it.

"Lucky Strike," he told me.

The Orange Section Magician

My grandfather ate oranges in sections.

He'd peel an orange, break it apart as nature intended, and line the sections on the kitchen table like wings on mounted butterflies. He'd chew one section at a time, holding the next section in front of his face. The sections would disappear, making him The Orange Section Magician.

The morning after the butter melted we had oranges for breakfast. Five oranges, with Norb Hike stopping by and eating two.

My grandfather was chewing his last orange section when Norb Hike broke the news about my grandfather's brand new Oldsmobile.

"I got a hundred and a half for it," he said, smiling.

My grandfather twitched, gagged, and wheezed, like a leashed schnauzer.

Darned Liquid, I thought.

My grandfather kept wheezing and coughing. My grandmother gave him the look she used on men who fainted at church.

Then she took her own bite of orange. "You gonna make it, *Stashu*?"

My grandfather raised his hand and nodded. He tried to speak but started coughing again. My grandmother took over as interpreter:

"A hundred fifty is all he'd give?" she asked Norb Hike.

"But he'll make your payments."

Cough, cough.

"We put *down* three hundred and a half."

"Her electrical was shot. I talked him up from eighty-five dollars first offer. Tops, he insisted."

Cough!

"*New*, the car was."

"A new lemon. With no hood. No boneyard has a new car hood. The hood he'll have to order direct from General Motors. And the butter in her trunk?"

Cough, cough.

"Twelve *dollars* worth of butter."

"To a baker worth twelve. This man sells cars, not babka. I tell you, Sophie, I got top dollar. Trust me."

My grandfather raised his hand. "Norb got top dollar," he said. "Why wouldn't he?"

My grandmother gave him her glare.

Norb Hike smiled. "Next Sunday I'll get yous a good used car." His pig nose moved up and down. "Used cars are like fish. Early Sunday morning's when you catch the keepers. We'll buy private, you know. You don't want to buy from no dealer. A dealer will take you. We'll buy private and get you a runner for less than the hundred and a half, title fee included. With the extra you'll have steaks for dinner."

This man can talk, I thought. He glanced at me and winked. I didn't wink back: I didn't know how.

My grandfather made a gun with his finger and thumb, put the barrel of it in his mouth.

"Caught back there?" my grandmother asked.

My grandfather nodded. His sinuses did a pretty good pig call. He cocked his thumb, his finger still in his mouth, aimed square at his brain.

This-Here-Malcolm

According to my grandmother, at one time my grandparents' basement was clean. With its red and black tile floor and a lifesize picture of costumed Polish dancers painted on one of its walls, it had been the sight of many Saturday night dances. Concertina Millie would bring her three piece band. Women living eight blocks past the firehouse brought their husbands. Cigar smoke hung like gauze curtains and my grandfather had to towel sweat off the floor between polkas.

"The time of our lives," my grandmother called it.

But as far as I remember, my grandparents' basement was box hell.

Everything they couldn't sell at the Seven Mile Fair was down there, in boxes.

I wasn't supposed to go there because it was too dangerous. You had to step over twenty-three shoe boxes on the stairs to get there, then reach behind a box the size of a telephone booth to flip on the light switch.

The one light that worked hung behind a box, so you could barely see the boxes everywhere else. There were boxes of used coat hangers, boxes of used egg cartons, boxes of used decorative soap decals, boxes of used bottle corks, boxes of used cigar boxes.

There was only one aisle: from the empty Ritz cracker boxes at the foot of the stairs to the toilet paper boxes on the far wall.

Other than that it was all boxes. Most were stacked to the ceiling, waiting for an earthquake.

One stack was five boxes of used colored Easter basket hay under a box of used bowling balls. I stayed away from that stack.

The first morning my grandfather went used car shopping, Anna was visiting. I was afraid of Anna those days because she always cried and I never knew what to say to her. But I still hadn't had breakfast that morning, so I walked into the kitchen.

Anna was sitting at the table, crying. My grandmother gave me the old stare. Anna pulled crumpled yellow kleenex from under the shoulder of her dress, blew her nose, honking like a park lagoon goose.

I looked in the breadbox: nothing. I stepped onto the back porch, where junk sat before it went in the basement.

"My Larry," Anna said. Then she went on, like a Good Friday church hymn:

> Larry, Larry, Larry.
> Oh God, My Larry.
> Larry, Larry.
> *Honk.*
> My Sweet Larry.
>
> (*Repeat.*)

It was worse than the smell of those Toni permanents.

I went outside to catch flies. That made things better until I realized the kitchen window was open:

"Did you hear this week? Chop meat just twelve cents a pound?"

"Twelve cents chop meat but no Larry to eat my meatloafs. *Honk.* Oh God. My sweet Larry."

So fly-catching was out. I plugged my ears, thought of a new thing to do: sneak in the basement and find the painting of the Polish dancers, which, according to my grandmother, was on the "sout" wall.

I crawled through the milk chute so my grandmother and Anna wouldn't hear the door open. I snaked beneath the crossfire of their words, wriggling belly-down toward the open basement door like a German under barbed wire on a battle-ground of linoleum.

Then I tiptoed over shoeboxes down the stairs, reaching the red and black tile floor unharmed.

The basement light was on: I didn't have to try to find the light switch and maybe knock down thirteen box stacks as if they were dominos.

I didn't know what "sout" meant, so I had to guess which wall the Polish dancers were probably buried against. I chose the far wall, which was somewhere behind the toilet paper boxes.

I was walking past the Easter-basket-hay-bowling-ball stack

as fast as I could when I heard footsteps and voices on the staircase:

"Watch how you step, hey. A few shoeboxes I have here until I make room for them. Trip and you'll go down on your *dupa.*"

"Or my head." *Honk.* "And join my Larry."

"Quit with the Larry. We've got egg cartons to find. We find and they're yours free. But don't tell my husband I gave you."

There was nothing to do except hide. But there were places for that. There were boxes.

I chose a long narrow box lying on its side with a picture of a four-man tent on it. The tent was the solid red color of box-print. An American family stood next to the tent: a blue grand-father taller than a red grandmother taller than a blue boy taller than a red girl.

I crawled in headfirst. There was no tent inside, just a few used toilet paper rolls my grandmother would make gifts out of someday. I had to nose right up to them to make sure my feet didn't show.

I heard no voices for awhile, just the sound of shoes against the tile floor, those black open-toed shoes 3P women wore because of old bunions.

Then the voices started again, less than a box-length away:

"I think he put them in this-here stack."

"This one?"

I felt cramped, like a cosmonaut.

"The one with your hand on it, hey. But in that middle box, I think."

"This-here?"

"Yeah."

"Ugh."

"Careful now. Watch those on top."

"Ugh. It don't feel like egg cartons. Feels like . . . Easter basket hay."

Easter basket hay?

"Try the bottom one," my grandmother said.

"This-here? Ugh."

"Watch it now."

"Help, hey."

"*Jesuz Kochani—*"

* * *

The used toilet paper rolls working like smelling salts, I came to in darkness. I first thought I was six feet under, buried in a used cardboard coffin. Then I remembered the American family and knew where I was.

I began wriggling out of the box but stopped when I heard voices:

"...and she's got the ten kids," Anna said. "You knew that, inna?"

"The Indian Lady has ten?" my grandmother said.

"Why sure."

"Ten I didn't know. I knew kids, but not ten."

"She's got that son. You've heard about the son, inna?"

"With the measles?"

"*Oh* no. Thirty-seven years old, this one is. Malcolm, I think she named him. You haven't heard?"

"I didn't know she had one that old."

"She probably wishes she didn't. You haven't *heard*? I shouldn't tell. I was sworn not to tell."

"*Tell.* It goes no further. I swear on my rosary here."

"Is your grandson upstairs listening maybe?"

"Gosh, no. He's out with his jar and his bugs."

"O.K. then. This-here Malcolm is thirty-seven years old, but nine of those he spent in Waupun."

"State Prison?"

"You never heard?"

"*Jesus* Lord no. For what did he spend nine years?"

"Your husband isn't home? This isn't for husbands."

Anna's voice faded. "Ask God's forgiveness for my talking, sweet Larry," she said, and then I couldn't hear her. I used the tips of my toes to push my tent box closer.

"What's this?" she said. "A box moving?"

"Where."

"On the floor there. Next to the bowling ball. Moving, it was."

My forehead began sweating.

"That-there one? *No.*"

"I saw it with my eyes."

"How would it move? We have no mice. Stanley puts out poison. Go ahead. He was hunting up north?"

"Hunting he was supposed to be when he meets this girl. Or better I should say *szkarada*. You've heard of these single girls up north during deer season, inna?"

"No."

"*Szkaradas*, all of them. And a drinker, this one."

"He too was a drinker?"

"Both of them drinkers. They're strangers drinking in this gin mill up north and he's throwing the darts."

"*Dress* darts?"

"No-no-no. The other kind. Like needles with feathers on the *dupa*? Thrown at circles on the wall? You've seen darts. Why sure you have. At Josaphat's hall they got the circles."

"Anyways."

"Anyways this-here Malcolm, he meets this *szkarada* playing darts. Him against she. And she beats him three times. He's champion four years straight down here—at the Eagles Club on the corner here by Schuster's?—and she beats him three times."

"So why to Waupun?"

"Because these two other fellas at this gin mill, coloreds I heard they were, ask to play next."

"Don't say coloreds. Did Christ say coloreds?"

"Christ *was* a colored. Someone told me that. Sister Flaviana, I think."

"Don't say coloreds. Say it proper. Society is advancing."

"Okay already. So this-here Malcolm keeps on with the darts, and the negrews challenge him and the *szkarada*."

"Challenge?"

"To the darts. But see the negrews, they wanna throw for money. Gamblers, these were. Now this-here Malcolm is no gambler, but he was champion four years straight down here by Schuster's, and the *szkarada* just beat him, so him and she play the negrews."

"For money?"

"Just nickels at first. But after Malcolm and she win some, it gets into dollars. Ten, twenty dollars a game, I heard."

"Holy Jaboli."

"And drinking the whole time—all of them. This goes on 'til two-three in the morning, when the *szkarada* starts throwing like a drunk girl. Ends up Malcolm loses three hundred dollars."

"*Oh* Lord. He made that kind of money?"

"No. He worked at Allen Bradley's. Third shift on the lathe. Forty dollars was all he had in his pocket."

"*All he had?* That's three weeks' groceries."

"But compared to what he owed? And these negrews, they want the money on the spot. Or Malcolm's car."

"New, his car was?"

"Used. But re*li*able."

"So let me guess. Malcolm takes a dart to the negrews."

"No. He gives the car. He doesn't want to owe to angry negrews. And the drunk *szkarada* drives him home. But to her trailer, she takes him. He's paying for his cabin but they go to her trailer. There they drink more highballs and start in with the whoopy."

"*No.*"

"Right there on her davenport."

"All this when he's there to shoot deer?"

"Honest to God."

"He wasn't married, no?"

"Three *years* at the time. With two little ones."

"Jesus Christmas."

"So he's in with the whoopy and there's knocks on the door. The *szkarada* gets up and answers in the nude. God's wrath if it's not one of them negrews—this-here Malcolm can see the dark skin through the doorway. The negrew is smiling and giving the *szkarada* cash money. And sweet-talking her. Sweet-talking and kissing."

"And a white girl she was? I can't even picture."

"Then she closes the door and comes back to her davenport there. This-here Malcolm, he asks who it was. My landlord, the *szkarada* sez. At four a.m. in the morning? Malcolm sez."

"And a *negrew* landlord?"

"That's exactly what he sez to her. He sez, What did this landlord want?"

"At four in the morning."

"That's what he *sez*! You heard this already?"

"Not a word. Go on with it."

"So the *szkarada* sez to him, He wanted my rental payment. Malcolm sez to her, Why did he give *you* cash if he wanted the rental? He gave no money, she sez. Malcolm sez to her, What's this-here in your hand? Nothing, she sez, but she drops something before she holds her hands out. This Malcolm, he sees that it's cash falling clear as day. But listen to this. He pretends he don't see it. And *f*inishes his whoopy."

"For God's *sake.*"

"When he's done he climbs off the davenport and sees ten dollars on the floor crumpled. He picks it up and puts it in his pocket and . . ."

"What."

"Murder."

"*No.*"

"Honest to God."

"Took a girl's life for ten dollars?"

"That's a week's groceries. Too, the girl was in on him losing his car."

"But *used*, it was."

"Re*li*able, I said."

"Don't say how he took her life. I don't even wanna hear."

"Fine by me. I'm sworn, remember."

"To who are you sworn."

"That I can't say."

"Not with his hunting knife, I hope."

"No."

"I don't even wanna know. I just hope not a shotgun."

"A lamp, he used."

"Jesus forgive our talking."

"Three times on the head, until the bottom part broke. They found bloody ceramic all over the floor there."

"And they arrested him?"

"A year later. I just saw that box move. Did you see movement?"

I froze. They're gonna catch me, I thought. Can a kid get arrested for hearing this?

"A rat it would take to move that box. We haven't rats. A year to arrest him?"

"For months they couldn't find him. Or the body."

"He confessed with a conscience?"

"No. A janitor found the girl's arm in a trashcan."

"Just the arm."

"Chopped at the elbow. With a ring on the finger."

"Married, she was?"

"Engaged."

"No."

"To the negrew."

"For Christ sakes."

"They'll do that now and then."

"Terrible. In her trailer park the janitor found it?"

"No. Behind an arch support factory near Sheboygan."

"I thought they hunted the deer north of Sheboygan."

"They do. This-here Malcolm, he chopped up the body and hid parts here and there all the way back to Milwaukee. After he stole his car back from the negrew, I mean. The other arm they found in Eau Claire. No ring on this one, but roughly the same length. Near Tomah they found a thighbone buried. Half her bosom a child found in Chippewa Falls in a lunch bag. They never found the head until after they arrested him up by Portage. There he lived secret for a year after he stopped home to get his clothes and toolchest."

"*Jesuz Kochani.* A criminal loose in the neighborhood."

"Why sure. And you know where they found the head?"

"Don't tell me."

"In his boxspring, the head. Wrapped in martinizing plastic and sewn in."

"And this was her Malcolm."

"Whose?"

"The Indian Lady's."

"Would I be sworn if he wasn't? Visit and you'll see him."

"I never visit. She always visits."

"And with reason. She don't want to have to explain him sitting there unemployed all day. You should visit. Dark glasses, he wears. At night, even."

The voices stopped—and I heard footsteps through the ceiling, my grandfather's.

Then the four open-toed shoes climbing the basement stairs and leaving the house.

Then a pair of high heels and voices: my grandfather's and a woman's—probably, I thought, Helen Pickadilly's.

For awhile I heard nothing.

Then the high heels leaving.

Then the squeaks and splashes of my grandfather washing his face.

Then my grandmother's open-toed shoes returning.

Then both my grandparents' voices, mostly my grandmother's.

After the door slammed and I knew they were looking for me outside, I made my move.

They found me in my grandmother's sewing-room, lying behind the fabric remnants on my burlap sack bed, facing the half-naked mannequin, eyes closed.

"Snoozing here all along," my grandmother said.

You could call it snoozing, I thought. But there's probably a better word.

"Sick," my grandfather said.

More Magic

My grandfather didn't buy a used car the day I learned about This-Here-Malcolm's Secret Body Parts Distributorship. Norb Hike didn't allow it.

"I just didn't get that feeling, Stanley," he said while eating my bullhead at dinner that night. "When I see your car, I'll get that feeling. Trust me."

It wasn't until the following Sunday morning that Norb Hike got that feeling.

I woke at dawn that day to the sound of my grandfather washing his face. After he made me dry the bathroom floor for him, a horn sounded outside, Norb Hike in an old car.

I walked outside. My grandfather followed, caught up, opened the passenger door—and we got in.

"Used?" my grandfather said.

"Twenty-nine Ford Model A two-door sedan," Norb Hike said, and he floored it. "A good runner."

The first used car my grandfather looked at was Larry's '49 Ford Tudor, in Anna's garage. Anna had left keys in her mailbox.

"She spends mornings talking with Ricky," Norb Hike explained, "but she's no early bird."

He had my grandfather open her garage door, then walked around the Tudor for five minutes. His lips stayed straight but the holes in his pig nose got wider.

"Good?" I asked him.

He didn't answer.

I thought about asking my grandfather, but he had his arms crossed: preventing twitches.

"Go ahead and start her," Norb Hike finally said.

My grandfather started her. She purred like a juice blender. My grandfather revved the engine: loud, louder, LOUDER—

Norb Hike waved his arms over his face. The garage went silent. "I don't get that feeling," he said. "Looks like this Larry let her sit quite a bit. Miles are low but a car sits and her ball joints go. You don't wanna buy with shot ball joints, Stanley. This ain't your car." He looked at me and winked.

His winking was beginning to make me wonder.

"Close the door," he said, and my grandfather obeyed faster than I could.

Norb Hike drove us past Pulaski Park to see a '51 Chevy. It was painted red over green and the owner smoked the first half-inch of four cigarettes during the test drive.

"Nope," Norb Hike said.

Norb Hike drove us past St. Josaphat's to see a '44 Buick.

It started rough and had a chipped windshield and bad rubber.

"Won't do," Norb Hike said.

Norb Hike drove us all the way to the North Side to see a '41 Cadillac. I had never been to the North Side before. The Cadillac had no heater and shimmied bad and was owned by a Puerto Rican man.

"We can do better," Norb Hike said.

Then Norb Hike drove us thirty-four miles south to some "property" outside of Kenosha. The property had a lot of acres, with trees standing everywhere, like soldiers. To get to the acre where the car was, we had to drive through a winding narrow path with low hanging tree branches that buffed the windshield like an automatic carwash.

Norb Hike's '29 Ford Model A made it through the branches without the windshield breaking, stopped on a farmhouse driveway. A German shepherd on the porch ran at us, barked and drooled, its tongue hanging like saltwater taffy. Norb Hike got out. The German shepherd jumped all over him as he grinned and looked at the farmhouse.

"Down, bitch," he said.

The German shepherd stopped jumping.

My grandfather got out of the car. The German shepherd began jumping all over him.

"Down," he said.

The German shepherd kept jumping.

Norb Hike looked over his shoulder. "Down, bitch," he said, and the German shepherd stopped jumping.

I rolled down my window. The German shepherd looked at me. "Don't bother, bitch," I said, and it followed my grand-father and Norb Hike around the side of the farmhouse.

I got out and followed all of them, like a caboose. Twenty-seven used cars sat behind the farmhouse, not many looking too good. Most were rusted over, their hoods yawning like parishioners.

Norb Hike walked from car to car, looking at their engines, shaking his head, smiling. "God damn," he said. He kept walking and smiling. He was looking at a burned car without doors or seats when a man chewing celery appeared from beside the farmhouse.

Liquid Johnny, I thought.

He wore a T-shirt and his real hair, the black slick version. He swallowed the celery but still had the arm with the bulldog tattoo. "Can I help you?" he said, like a farmer.

"Maybe," Norb Hike said.

I ran to my grandfather's side, pointed at Liquid Johnny.

"He's a dealer," I said. "You don't want to buy from a dealer."

Liquid Johnny looked at me as if I were a window between him and a naked redhead.

Norb Hike's shiny forehead wrinkled. "You a dealer?" he asked Liquid Johnny.

Liquid Johnny shook his head. "Grow corn and beans is what I do. Bought the property with these cars sittin' on it."

I pointed at the bulldog tattoo. "That's the man who got us the tow truck."

My grandfather looked at the bulldog.

"You run a towing operation?" Norb Hike said.

"Tractor is all I run."

My grandfather looked at me. "Gray hair, the man who got the tow truck had," he said. He cupped his hand around my ear and whispered so loud it tickled: "Let Norb do the talking. He knows the business."

I had done all I could. There was nothing to do but try to smile, watch, and learn.

My mouth wouldn't smile but Norb Hike led my grandfather, Liquid Johnny and me from car to car until we came to a silver and gray one.

"'33 Pontiac," he said.

The '33 Pontiac had smooth tires and a puddle of brown water under the pedals. Shoulder-high grass was growing through a hole in the floor.

Liquid Johnny took a pocket knife to the carburetor to get it started. It coughed black smoke and bounced. When Norb

Hike put it in gear, it jumped.

My grandfather and I got in. Norb Hike drove in circles around the clearing like a ringleader. The front end squeaked until he turned on the radio full blast. "NO STATIC," he said, then stopped on the oval of oil-stained grass the car had hidden. He turned off the ignition.

The engine coughed six times, hissed, and got quiet.

"Only thirty-four thousand on her, Stanley," Norb Hike said. "That's nothing on a car this old."

Liquid Johnny sat on the hood of the car with his hands in his pockets, staring at the farmhouse.

"Let's check the accessories," Norb Hike said. He turned to my grandfather. "Roll up the windows."

We rolled up the windows.

"I had you do that so we could talk," he said.

I watched Liquid Johnny through the cracked windshield while they talked:

"I got that feeling," Norb Hike said.

"For this-here one?"

"Sure. She needs a little work, but I got that feeling. This is your car, Stanley. This is it."

My grandfather spread his legs: grass.

"That hole we can patch with cardboard," Norb Hike said. "I got plenty a that at the worm farm. Won't cost you a penny. There's nothing here we can't fix ourselves. Cars you can fix yourself make the best deals. See this farmer don't know we can fix it. To him it's a jalopy. I'll talk him down. It's a runner, Stanley. I got that feeling. This is your best used car. Trust me."

"You got that feeling?"

"Through and through. I got a nose for a good used car, Stanley. This is yours."

"You can talk him down?"

"I'll get her for fifty. She's worth the hundred and a half but I'll get her for a third of that. You watch me."

"She's worth a hundred and a half?"

"Sure. Your older cars run forever. They don't make 'em like this anymore."

"I like the color. Gold is my favorite but I also like silver."

"And a darn sharp silver, Stanley. I tell you what. Hold my wallet for now."

My grandfather took Norb Hike's wallet.

"Give me fifty of your dollars."

My grandfather gave him fifty dollars.

"We'll make like I'm buying for myself with only fifty in my pocket. If we have to offer a little higher, we'll make like you're borrowing me money. This way he thinks I can't afford much more than fifty."

We got out of the car. The German shepherd walked up to my grandfather, nuzzled the zipper of his pants. My grandfather twitched. Then Norb Hike and Liquid Johnny talked, Norb Hike like a car dealer and Liquid Johnny like a farmer.

While we watched them, my grandfather took out his handkerchief and blew his nose. He gave it all he had, then held the handkerchief open a foot away from his face. He raised an eyebrow and lowered his hands so I could see: an orange section, the same one he'd choked on days before.

The Orange Section Magician had struck again.

But so did Liquid Johnny and Norb Hike.

Because when the talking was over, my grandfather had bought a '33 Pontiac for $157.

Norb Hike lent him the extra seven.

The car had 234,689 miles on it, but my grandfather didn't know that then.

The Limping Chihuahua

My grandfather had a 3P auto mechanic, Joe Zwolinski. Joe had black grease under his fingernails, teeth so rotten you wanted to take a pliers to them, and a purple blood blister on a different finger every time I saw him.

I saw him whenever my grandfather took me to get his '33 Pontiac off the rack.

I saw the points and condenser blister, the U-joint blister, the brakes-all-the-way-around blister, the overhauled transmission blister, the master cylinder blister, and the rebuilt engine blister.

Actually I never quite saw the rebuilt engine blister.

My sixth birthday arrived during the rebuilt engine blister.

I woke that morning to the sound of my grandfather washing his face. I looked at my grandmother's mannequin—which wore nothing but a white robe—and yawned. Then I remembered it was my day.

I got up, stepped around some dress patterns and pin cushions, walked past my grandfather and the wet bathroom floor, then looked in the kitchen. Sitting on the table was my birthday present, a used shoebox wrapped in a *Milwaukee Journal* Sunday comics section and used tomato bush twine.

I opened it carefully—so my grandparents could re-use the paper and yarn. Inside were three pieces of hard bubble gum, a cap gun without caps, and a cracked water pistol.

I thought about using the water pistol on my grandfather until he walked into the kitchen towelling his wet neck and shoulders.

"Grandma went shopping with the Indian Lady," he said.

I expected those to be his only words of the day, but was wrong:

"Pears are three cents a pound, limit twenty pounds. I wanted them to take you and get extra but Grandma said no.

She told me let him sleep. I go now to Lincoln Avenue Garage and pay Joe. You stay here and behave."

That was almost a sermon, I thought. The man is losing his mind.

I figured he'd used up his entire life's word allowance, but was wrong again:

"And no snooping in the basement."

He turned and went to my grandparents' bedroom. I heard him open the top drawer of his cardboard dresser, his money drawer, the one I couldn't reach. When he returned to the kitchen he was wearing Old Spice cologne and an orange Hawaiian shirt with Birds of Paradise on it. I'd smelled Old Spice on Norb Hike before but never on my grandfather. And I'd never seen that Birds of Paradise shirt, either.

"Fancy," I said.

He walked toward the back door smoothing back his hair with his Swedish steel comb, pinky extended. He never mentioned my birthday and his goodbye was the jingling of his keys as he locked me in.

When the jingling stopped I made my own breakfast, ketchup bread. Ketchup bread is nothing fancy, a slice of bread covered with ketchup.

I ate the ketchup bread and went straight for the basement.

I walked down and up the stairs three times, to show who was boss. Then I started digging out the Polish dancer wall painting.

I moved thirty-seven boxes and *saw* it: the painted arm of a Polish dancer stretched across the wall like a tree branch.

Five more boxes and the Polish dancers were free. I stood back and looked. The man wore baggy black pants and a black vest with a peacock on it. The woman wore red ribbons in her hair and a white dress that was beginning to whirl up over her head. They stood side by side. Their outside arms were raised like professional singers.

The woman was smiling.

The man was smiling and winking.

One his hands was behind her.

What's going on back there? I thought, then realized that the woman's face looked a little like Pam Hike's.

I hummed "Somewhere Over the Rainbow" three times.

Then I re-stacked the boxes, went upstairs, and left the house through the milk chute. I was doing the only thing left to do: find the Indian Lady's house and lay eyes on This-Here-Malcolm. I'd never been to the Indian Lady's house but knew she lived across from Pulaski Park: past the firehouse, past Helen Pickadilly's used sweet shop, almost as far as Joe Zwolinski's Lincoln Avenue Garage.

I took the alley route to avoid my grandfather. The firetruck was doing its little sniffing routine and there were no used police cars parked behind Helen Pickadilly's sweet shop.

It was This-Here-Malcolm or bust.

When I heard the shouts of about thirteen children, I sensed I was onto something. A dark-skinned kid chased a limping Chihuahua across the cobblestone ahead of me and I thought, Must be close.

I crept from ashcan to ashcan until I was crouched behind a smelly one that belonged to what had to be the Indian Lady's house, a three story bungalow covered by a patches of shingled siding. Some of the shingles were green, some were pink, some were brown, some were whitewashed, some were torn off. There were five clotheslines strung across the back yard clothespinned to sixty-four pieces of underwear flapping in the wind like flags.

The underwear was all different sizes. Thirteen kids with dark skin and black eyes chased the limping Chihuahua through the clothesline aisles, screaming.

"Kids," I whispered. I pictured the Indian Lady sitting inside the house, on her toilet. When the wind blew the underwear just right, I saw her back porch. There was a card table on it, and, sitting on a folding chair behind the card table, a dark-haired man in mirrored sunglasses. The folding chair was leaned back against a patch of green shingled siding and his legs were on the card table, crossed at the ankles. He held a harmonica to his mouth with both hands but I couldn't hear it, with the thirteen kids screaming at that Chihuahua to beat hell.

"This-Here-Malcolm," I whispered.

The wind blew the underwear and I saw him again. Then a siren went off. He didn't move but the kids ran from the yard like scared rabbits. They passed my ashcan without seeing me and shot up the alley toward the firehouse. The limping Chihuahua followed. The kids' shouts faded and I heard This-Hear-Malcolm's harmonica but the wind died and I couldn't see him. He was playing "The Church's One Foundation," accompanied by the siren.

When the siren stopped he played "The Church's One

Foundation" alone. I listened and watched the underwear not move. Then I decided to leave, to beat my grandfather home.

I took the alley, walking toward what was becoming a crowd of Indian kids and neighbor ladies standing behind Helen Pickadilly's garage—close to where the used police car had been the day I saw the front of her sweetshop.

When I reached the crowd, I saw a firetruck parked in the street alongside her garage. The firehouse across from the front of her sweetshop was empty, meaning the firemen had probably circled the block a few times before stopping.

American heroes, I thought. The Indian kids and twenty-six neighbor ladies stood whispering to one another, pointing at the back of Helen Pickadilly's sweetshop. The Chihuahua stood on three legs, panting. I stood next to the Chihuahua. An ambulance rounded the corner and stopped alongside the firetruck.

Two ambulance men took a stretcher from the ambulance and entered the sweetshop through the front, like people were supposed to. Then the Indian Lady showed up, without my grandmother or This-Here-Malcolm. She stood next to me but never looked at me.

Eight minutes later a fireman opened the back door. Women and children, I realized, were looking inside the back room of Helen Pickadilly's sweetshop. I saw incense sticks burning in a crystal vase, a purse on a nightstand, and a giant unmade bed.

Then it happened:

The ambulance men brought out the stretcher.

A man lay on it, almost naked. A bloody handtowel covered his face. His hands covered the hairy place where his legs met.

They put him in the ambulance and someone appeared behind the screen of the back door, Helen Pickadilly in her white robe, a Birds of Paradise shirt hung over her shoulder.

Everyone—including the Indian kids—got quiet. The Indian Lady walked up to the screen door, stood face to face with Helen Pickadilly for four minutes, then walked back to the alley. The other neighbor ladies gathered around her.

The Indian Lady began whispering.

The Indian kids tried to listen. While the Indian Lady shooed them away, I stepped directly behind her. The other neighbor ladies were too busy listening to see me.

"... she said he was a helper," the Indian Lady was saying in her eye-rolling tone of voice.

"*Hel*per?" a neighbor lady said.

The Indian Lady wiped sweat from her mustache. "A fix-it man, she told me. Helping her fix her toaster, she said."

"A cracked skull fixing a toaster? You'd think electrocution, but not a cracked skull. And why naked? *Naked*, and fixing a toaster?"

"The firemen took his clothes off, she told me."

"Naked and a cracked skull. That's some helper she had. Did she say how the skull cracked?"

"Slipped on a wet floor, she told me."

"A floor wet while fixing a toaster?"

"*After* fixing the toaster, she said. She said he slipped on tile in the bathroom."

The neighbor ladies looked at their feet, made signs of the cross, whispered fast prayers. One of them glared at the Indian Lady. "In the *bath*room he fixed the toaster?"

"She said he fixed the toaster in her kitchen. In her bathroom he washed his face."

"He must have washed his face like a crazy man."

"Like an elephant in a bird bath, she told me."

Something screamed: the ambulance driver was revving his engine in neutral. The ambulance itself began rolling, toward streets I'd never seen. Its siren was silent. Its red lights flickered like twitches.

Three Story Bungalow

That 4th of July I was in a parade: my grandfather's funeral procession. My grandmother, the wooden coffin and I rode in the first car, a used hearse. Bruno A. Pruski was driving. I stared at the mirror outside my window: twelve stiff flags on car antennas, little purple flags with white words on them:

B. PRUSKI FUNERAL

We stopped in St. Stanislaus Cemetery. The sky was low and gray, the bark on the oak trees damp. People got out of their used cars and walked over soggy sod to a pile of dirt next to a hole.

There weren't any nice purple tombstones nearby, just crosses made from used fence pickets. The nice purple tombstones were across the creek. Six kids stood in the creekbed, watching us.

My grandmother and I stood near the hole. Joan Hike and sixteen old 3Ps stood around us. Four women wore black dresses my grandmother had sewn and sold to them at a profit. The Indian Lady's heels were sinking into the sod. Helen Pickadilly stood behind everyone.

Bruno A. Pruski dropped an armload of red, white and blue carnations on the dirt pile. "Where's little Pam?" my grandmother asked Joan Hike.

"Singing."

Where's big Gertie? I wondered.

My grandmother nodded down a burp: summer sausage. Norb Hike and five old 3P men I'd never seen before set the wooden coffin next to the hole. One old man had long-john frosting and poppy seeds between his nostrils. Father Pat made the sign of the cross and everyone looked at the cut wet grass on their shoes. The Indian Lady's heels were gone.

"Our Father who art in heaven—"

BANG!

The kids ran from the creek bed, hid behind the biggest purple tombstones.

"That was no cap gun," Norb Hike said.

"Hallowed be they name. Thy kingdom come—"

BANG!

"That was at least an M-8O."

A young man with a big chin and rubber boots walked out of a house behind the good tombstones shaking his finger at the kids. They ran away in zigzags, like pinballs.

". . . but deliver us from evil. Amen."

"FFFfff," my grandmother farted.

Norb Hike and the five old men looped two pieces of clothesline around the coffin and began lowering it into the hole. Joan Hike looked at my grandmother. "Ten dollars cheaper that way," my grandmother said. The coffin went lower and lower.

"My back's giving," Norb Hike said. "It gave," he said louder, and his end of the coffin hit mud.

The other end stuck out of the hole. An old man without frosting wiped his nose with his palm. "Does it have to be flush against the bottom, hey?"

Norb Hike squeezed his back, nodded.

The three oldest men got on their knees and grabbed the end of the coffin that was sticking out.

"Heave," Norb Hike said. "Use your legs."

SPLAT.

"For God's *sake*," my grandmother said.

A clear drop hung from Helen Pickadilly's jaw. She touched her eyes with a rouge-stained handkerchief. Her mouth looked crooked. Everyone else had straight lips and dry faces.

Father Pat read from a book with a purple ribbon in it. We all said "Lord, hear our prayer" nine times. Finally people began leaving.

My grandmother, Joan Hike and the Indian Lady stayed.

"Go say good-bye to your grandfather," my grandmother said.

I stepped to the edge of the hole, stared at the red, white and blue carnations, heard something tear through the leaves on the oak tree branches above me.

A Roman candle landed on the carnations. I picked it up, looked at the directions:

EMITS A SHOWER OF SPARKS.
LIGHT AND GET AWAY.

". . . can't afford feeding him," I heard Joan Hike say.

My grandmother nodded, turned to the Indian Lady and whispered something. I pretended to look at more directions, which were written in Chinese.

"If he does his chores," the Indian Lady said, and my grandmother nodded.

Finally I realized what they were planning. At first I didn't mind. Then I thought, *This-Here-Malcolm!* He'll kill me, butcher me, and throw my thigh in an ashcan.

"He needs to be around kids," my grandmother said.

"Send him right over," the Indian Lady said. "I got lawnwork needs to be done."

I dropped the Roman candle and my grandmother and I walked home. She put half my clothes in a used paper bag. I was wearing the other half. She put my toothbrush behind my ear. "You'll live with the Indian Lady now," she told me, and patted the top of my head. "I'll still be your grandmother."

Until This-Here-Malcolm gets me, I almost said, but didn't—because I'd been in the basement when I'd heard about him.

My grandmother would have twisted my ear off for that.

I adjusted my toothbrush and she rolled the bag closed. "Tell her keep the bag. For that black tread she borrowed me."

I took the bag and walked up the alley until I saw the Indian Lady's three-story bungalow: my new multi-colored home. Loose tarpaper flapped in the wind. All the Indian kids except This-Here-Malcolm were on their hands and knees in the backyard. Lawnwork? I thought, because there was was no lawn on their backyard, just trampled-hard dirt and muddy water in a hole the size of Volkswagen.

The hole was their homemade pond. They were building little limestone driveways and planting elm tree twigs around the shoreline. Their black hair was short as eyelashes: boys, girls, it didn't matter. The Chihuahua stood on three legs, watching.

A turtle shell peeling like taffy wrappers sat on an inner tube floating in the pond. An orange inner tube patch blew bubbles into the water. Harmonica music came from somewhere upstairs in the bungalow. I didn't recognize the melody: a This-Here-Malcolm original.

I set my clothes bag on the trampled-hard dirt, stood behind the Indian kids. Some looked at me without talking. The others kept working. I felt like the tarpaper.

"Go get the hose," one finally said to me. He was kneeling beside me, planting an elm tree twig.

"Who are you?" I said.

"Joey. The oldest out here. Go get the hose."

Joey had long fingernails with dirt under them: tiny shovels. A jagged scar connected his ear to the outside corner of his eye and a chewed-up toothpick hung from his lip.

He scratched his scarred eye corner with his longest dirty fingernail. "Get the *hose*."

I walked to the side of the house, where the hose had been at my grandparents'.

"No, dummy," he yelled. "In the basement."

I headed for the back door.

"*God*," he yelled. He looked at the other Indian kids. "Someone show him."

"You show him," a girl's voice said.

Joey grabbed a rusty garden spade flyswatter style. It had a half-cracked-off handle. "*Show* him, Diezee."

A skinny girl rose like toast. She had brown skin and wore a shirt cut from feed sack burlap. According to the faded blue lettering on her sleeve, she weighed fifty pounds. Her baggy corduroys, safety pinned at the navel and frayed at the heel, walked toward me with her hands on their hips. She was Diezee.

"The basement's over *there*," she said, pointing at the first stormdoor I'd ever seen. She walked back to the pond.

The stormdoor looked like a trapdoor to hell but I went and lifted it anyway. It was heavy as a concrete slab and slammed open against the trampled-hard dirt.

The harmonica music stopped. Joey rolled his eyes without looking at me. The harmonica music began, and I walked down the stairs.

The basement was dark, cool and smelled like dill weed. I couldn't see. I put my hands in front of my face, took a step, then tripped and fell on the dirt floor. It was hard but not as trampled as the backyard. I saw what I'd tripped on: a toy dump truck with a bad front end.

I looked around. Broken toy car parts covered the floor like a plane crash: toy tires, toy chasses, toy steering wheels, toy parts I'd never seen before. There were also broken doll parts: doll legs, doll arms, hollow doll stomachs, bald doll heads with gouged-out eyes.

The harmonica music got louder. "You haven't *found* it?" a voice said.

Diezee was standing on the concrete stairs, a square of blue daylight behind her. Her hands were still on her hips. It was good seeing some connected female body parts.

"I was looking at this dump truck," I said.

"The hose is right *there*," she said, pointing to the basement's darkest corner.

"I know. Why all the doll parts?"

"They're just parts. Garbage."

"You should put some together."

"Can't. No arms and legs match. Hurry up with the hose. We're 'posed to empty the pond and get the rotted baloney out before Ma smells it. Or she'll make us fill it in and plant tomatoes."

"What's baloney doing in a pond?"

"Turtle food. Our turtle leaves scraps."

I went and grabbed the hose. A snake slid out the end, fell to the floor, slithered past a doll neck and into the harmonica music.

I felt myself almost twitch. "Scared me," I said instead. That made me glad: I wanted to be a talker like Norb Hike instead of a twitcher like my dead grandfather.

"Just a garter snake," Diezee said. "They don't bite or nothing. Just stink up your hand when you hold them too long."

"What's it doing here?"

"Joey caught a pregnant one at the tracks. She escaped from her cage, right between the popsicle sticks. That was two years ago. Her grandkids are everywhere now. *Hurry.*"

I shook the hose a good one: there was nothing up my sleeve and I wanted to keep it that way. I followed Diezee toward the daylight, pulling the hose to the pond.

Joey was kneeling and patting dirt around his elm tree twig, which stood like a First Holy Communicant. "Gimme."

I gave him the hose. He put the end in the muddy water. A head poked out of the turtle shell, then four feet, the back ones paddling wildly. Claws caught the inner tube and the shell slid in the water like a coin into a slot.

"You did it *again*, Fommy," Joey said.

I thought he was calling me Fommy. I looked at my corrective shoes. My feet didn't need correcting, but a German had traded the shoes to my grandfather for 24O balloons.

"I didn't either," a kneeling medium-sized Indian kid said: Fommy. He had dark skin and snot the color of pie crust.

I was glad I wasn't Fommy.

"You did *too*," Joey said.

"I didn't *either*."

Joey stood on his knees and lifted the garden spade fly swatter style.

Fommy looked like a fly until he closed a nostril with a finger, aimed it at Joey, and snotted. Joey ducked. A paste-colored snot hit the trampled-hard dirt like dough on linoleum. Joey swung the garden spade and Fommy ducked, covering his face with his arm.

"Strike one," he said.

Joey swung again: CLONK, like spoon against cantaloupe, but louder. The Chihuahua lifted its nose and howled. It didn't have teeth. A few Indian kids looked up from their work.

"Foul ball?" Joey said.

"Fair," Fommy said with his arm over his face. "You win." He dropped his arm, blinked six times, shrugged his shoulders. Then the skin between his eyebrows wrinkled and his lower lip stiffened and he pressed his eyes with his brown thumb and finger, shoulders bouncing.

Joey dropped the garden spade. The other Indian kids kept working. The Chihuahua limped to the snot, sniffed it, limped back to the pond.

"Go suck the other end," Joey said.

I watched Fommy. I felt sorry for him but wanted to hear the garden spade hit his head again. He sat back on his heels, eyes closed.

"You hear me?" Joey said.

Fommy's shoulders kept bouncing. I turned to Joey, who was looking at me. He didn't grab the garden spade but his fingers inched closer to the cracked-off handle.

"I didn't know you were talking to me," I said.

"*Stu*pid. When we siphon the pond, whoever gets the hose has to suck the other end. Hurry. Before Ma comes."

There was no arguing with a guy who used words like

"siphon." I ran to the stormdoor. The other end of the hose was hanging off the fourth step down. I grabbed it and sucked, tasting grass, brass and rubber.

Joey grabbed the garden spade and stood. "KEEP SUCKING."

I sucked again.

"HARDER."

I sucked harder.

"SUCK!"

I sucked so hard my lungs burned. Joey began walking toward me. The garden spade's edges looked sharp. I gave the hose my best sucking effort. Then came the explosion, filling my mouth almost up to my eyes. It tasted muddy, but I swallowed as much as I could.

A chunk of rotten baloney came through and Joey yanked the hose from my mouth. "Ya don't *swallow* it, dummy," he said. "Haven't you ever *siphoned* anything before?"

Water from the hose ran down the basement stairs.

"No."

Joey led me back to the pond. I chewed the baloney chunk. Fommy lay on his back with his arms folded. The other Indian kids lay stomach-down around the shoreline watching the water level drop. The Chihuahua licked its bad leg. One Indian kid's tennis shoes didn't have soles.

The baloney chunk felt like old gum, so I swallowed it.

"Don't anyone touch the hose," Joey said.

There was new, clear snot around Fommy's nostrils, a streak like dried glue on his forearm, and a bump the size of a bottle cap on his hairline.

No one said anything. The water level dropped, reached the turtle's shell, began boiling with wriggling flashes of silver and orange.

"NOW!" Joey yelled, and the Indian kids grabbed at the water like 3P women at a yarn clearance sale. Joey looked at me. "GRAB!"

I faked a few grabs to keep him happy. The Indian kids were coming up with handfuls of goldfish, newts, and tadpoles. I grabbed for real, came up with a crayfish and a slimy chunk of bologna. Diezee took the crayfish.

Soon Joey had two goldfish bigger than crappie upside-down in his hands. Their red gills were wide open, hoping for rain. "Get the *residue!*" he said—another word you couldn't argue with. I grabbed with both hands. "Residue" felt slimy. When my hands broke the surface, I gagged.

Joey squeezed both big goldfish. Their eyes bulged, aimed at his long fingernails. "RUN THE NEW WATER!"

I ran to the basement squeezing juice from the residue. I dropped the pulp in a toy truck bed, pulled the end of the hose to the faucet, and screwed it onto the spigot with hands that trembled like a gearshift in neutral: I didn't want Joey's goldfish to end up floating. I turned on the faucet, ran back to the pond.

The water level rose. The Indian kids put their handfulls back in. You could see animals in action now: swimming, crawling, nipping each other. I stared at them and listened to the harmonica music. It stopped. I looked up. The Indian kids were ganged up around the open back door, oozing through the doorway like a last squeeze of toothpaste. Diezee and Fommy were at the end of the line. Fommy aimed a nostril her way, went in before her. I was almost alone now, which would be fine.

Then the harmonica began playing again: alone *wouldn't* be fine. I grabbed my clothes bag and ran to the back door. Diezee was holding it open, smiling with a tooth missing.

A short hall with scuffed walls was connected to the back doorway. We were all packed into it. The Indian kids were kicking off their shoes and running into the next room. The kid without soles didn't bother. Diezee was the last shoe-kicker. I followed her into the next room, the kitchen.

The Indian Lady stood at the gas-burning stove pouring elbow macaroni into a steaming pot. God, she was big. A drop of sweat hung from the tip of her nose like water from toilet pipes.

"You take off your shoes?" she said. She didn't look at us, just tried to tongue the sweat drop as it dove into the pot.

"Yeah," Diezee said, and she ran into the next room. I returned to the hall to kick off my shoes, afraid that Diezee would disappear somewhere and leave me alone with the Indian Lady. Corrective, I thought as I kicked off my shoes. Still too big, they scuffed the wall.

I walked back through the kitchen. The harmonica was louder.

The Indian Lady lifted her head like a turtle. "You scuff the wall?"

"No."

I put my clothes bag on the table. "My grandmother said to keep the bag. For the tread."

The Indian Lady stared at her boiling elbow macaroni. "Tread?"

"The black tread you borrowed her."

"Oh, *sewing* tread."

I ran into the next room. It was big and missing chunks from the ceiling. The floor was covered with carpet samples the Indian Lady had bought from my dead grandfather: most mustard brown, some pink, all worn and dirty from grease, gum and shoeprints. A big wooden television set stood against the wall with no screen in it, just Diezee and Fommy pretending to be on television. They used a ball peen hammer for a microphone. Diezee's pants were unzipped.

"Leave us alone," Fommy said.

"Where's everyone else?" I asked.

"We can't hear you," Diezee said. "We're on television."

"You don't have to hear me. I just have to hear you. Just tell me where everyone else is."

"Are you afraid of my mom?" Fommy said.

"No."

"You afraid of my oldest brother?"

"No."

"That's where everyone else is. With my oldest brother. In the attic. Just go upstairs and climb the ladder in the hall." He pointed at stairs near the kitchen doorway.

I had three choices: stay there and look like a liar, go to the kitchen and watch the Indian Lady boil elbow macaroni, or go upstairs and get killed by This-Here-Malcolm. Talkers like Norb Hike never look like liars, I thought. And I'd rather die than watch the Indian Lady. I headed for the stairs.

They were carpeted with different colored samples and covered with plastic. The walls had crayon drawings all over them, red stick people with balloons attached to their mouths.

The balloons contained words: "WELCOME HOME MALCOLM." The harmonica music got louder. I was in a hallway now, good old linoleum. A hamster ran across it.

A rope ladder hung from a hole in the ceiling. This hole, I thought, is no missing chunk. It was square, went all the way through. The harmonica music was clear, loud, up there.

I climbed the ladder, poked my head through the hole. The harmonica music stopped. The air was hot and smelled like the upholstery of Larry's '49 Ford Tudor. There was no light except for a long box of sunlight from a tiny square window.

"You here to see the squirrel monkey?" a soft voice said. There was a mattress beneath the sunlight: no box spring, no sheets, just pillows, seven pillows. This-Here-Malcolm was lying among them wearing boxer shorts and black sunglasses. His red hair was greased back and dark as dried blood. He held a harmonica as if it were a ham sandwich. There was a glow-in-the-dark crucifix on the wall behind him, a stack of thick magazines at his feet. His bony thighs squeezed a sweating brown bottle of Pabst.

"Fommy said everyone was up here," I said.

"You, me, and a squirrel monkey," he said. "Is that everyone?" His voice was calm but frightening, like Father Pat's.

"You keep a *monkey* up here?"

"Thing's been living in those rafters for four years. Ever since it got out of its cage. Too fast to catch."

Even in boxer shorts and sunglasses, This-Here-Malcolm seemed like a nice enough guy. He won't kill you, I thought. He might cut your thumb off, but he won't kill you. "What's he eat?"

"Sunflower seeds. Eats them out of that bowl on the floor when I'm asleep. I never actually seen him eat, but the seeds are always gone in the morning."

"Where'd you get him?"

"Sent out for him when I was a kid. You've seen the ads in comic books."

I'd never seen a comic book. I stared at This-Here-Malcolm.

"You know," he said. "'Squirrel monkeys, $16.99 postpaid.' Another five bucks if you want it insured. I sent in $16.99— couldn't wait to save up the insurance money. Six weeks later a box came with a dead monkey inside. Stiff. They *sent* that thing dead. So I saved up and sent $21.99. A box with holes in it came with this one. To tell you the truth, I wish they'd have sent him dead also. I could use twenty bucks right now."

"Why don't you just quit feeding him?"

This-Here-Malcolm sat up, swigged some Pabst, lifted his sunglasses off his nose. His eyes were tiny and black, like wet rosary beads. "'Cause starvation ain't enough for that thing." His eyes seemed to shrink. "I wanna *maul* the little bastard."

I took a step down the rope ladder.

"Where you going?" he said. His eyes pinned me stiff.

"Nowhere."

"You're that Stanley guy's grandkid, aren't you."

"Yeah."

"He's dead, isn't he."

"Yeah."

He dropped his glasses back on his nose and crawled on his hands and knees to the edge of his bed, three feet away from me. His harmonica was still in his hand and a stream of saliva reversed itself down his wrist.

"Your dad is dead, too, isn't he."

"*Dad?*"

"Your father."

"Father Pat?"

"No. A married guy. A guy married to your mom."

"Mom?"

"Your mother."

"You mean grandmother?"

"No. Just *mother*. Younger than your grandmother."

"I don't have one of those."

"Not now, but you used to. You had a father, too. They died when you were little. Your mother died of scarlet fever. Your father died during a test drive. He sold used cars."

Used cars! I thought. "Says who?"

"Says your grandmother. She told my mother."

"Who's your mother?"

"The lady downstairs. Cooking."

"I thought that was your grandmother."

"My grandmother's dead. That's how it's supposed to happen. Your grandparents die when you're little. Your parents die when you're big. Your situation, little man, got reversed."

This-Here-Malcolm sat on the edge of his bed. I was eye-level with his feet and he had the largest big toe I'd ever seen. "You ever see a dead person?" he said.

"Yeah."

"Your grandfather?"

"Yeah. And a man named Larry."

"You ever go hunting?"

Something moist grabbed my ankle. I looked down: a hand, Indian brown. "Get down here," a man's voice said—the Indian Lady's.

I climbed down the rope steps until we were face to face. She looked at me for the first time ever. Her lips were straight and tight. So were mine. She hooked her finger around my belt loop, carried me down the staircase and through the television room and kitchen, then set me on my feet in the short hall leading to the backdoor. She grabbed the back of my neck like an adjustable wrench and put my face so close to the scuff marks I smelled leather.

"YOU DO THIS?"

I kept my lips straight.

She nodded my head, grabbed my wrist, dragged me outside and into the basement. A clear bright light bulb hung from the ceiling. She aimed my face at the residue in the toy truckbed, squeezed my neck in adjustable wrench fashion.

"YOU DO *THIS?*"

She nodded my head again, grabbed a doll leg, and spanked me seventeen times with its ass end.

"No dinner for you tonight. You stay down here and clean up. Until I say otherwise." She left and slammed the storm door, then locked it behind her.

Some mother, I thought. I sat under the light bulb, on a doll head, staring at a smashed toy convertible.

Father, I thought, wondering if what This-Here-Malcolm had said about parents was true.

And then, for the first time ever, it happened:

My throat began tightening. My face felt hot. Water filled my eyes, ran warm down my cheeks, hung in cool drops from my chin.

A drop fell to the dirt floor and I remembered my grandmother saying "used cars" at the Hike's—and how everyone got quiet and no one, not even Pam Hike, looked at me.

My shoulders began bouncing—like Fommy's had. Father, I thought, and my throat closed itself tighter still. Hot water refilled my eyes. My shoulders bounced harder and harder.

The Authorities

The floor was cold: October. I was sleeping in the kitchen now, under the table with dustballs and a hard piece of toast. I dreamt pressure, felt pain, woke up: the Indian Lady was stepping on my hand. I yanked it from under her. She twisted, thumped stomach-first onto the floor, grabbed her ankle, rocked on her back flab like a wooden horse. Linoleum squeaked. Her face turned red. Six Indian kids came running.

"It's just Ma."

"I thought the refrigerator tipped over."

The Indian Lady's ankle got bigger and darker. She shook her finger at me. "From now on you sleep with Fommy."

The Indian kids pointed: "HA-HA-HA-HA-HA! HA-HA-HA-HA-HA!"

I looked at the floor, kept my lips straight.

"HA-HA-HA-HA—"

"And no breakfast for anyone."

The Indian kids shut up.

The Chihuahua licked the Indian Lady's ankle. She backhanded it across the floor and looked at me. "It rained last night."

"I know."

"Front sidewalk needs shovelling."

"I understand," I said—though I didn't. "Where's the shovel?"

"Sneak it from the neighbor's garage," Joey said.

I did that. Then I walked in front of the Indian Lady's three-story bungalow, to see what needed to be shovelled. Her front lawn was a hill like my grandmother's, but steeper and without grass on it, the sidewalk below covered with purple-gray mud.

Joey stood in the mud with a storm window under his arm. He walked backwards into the street, lifted the storm window over his head, ran at the hill, got halfway up, fell on his face and slid down. "Shit."

A kid my size and color was walking down the sidewalk across the street, kicking elm leaves. He had something under his arm. I pointed. "Why is he carrying hymnals around?"

Joey turned. "Those aren't hymnals." He cupped a muddy hand around his mouth: "FOOL, FOOL. YOU GOTS TO GO TO SCHOOL!"

The kid ran away.

"Those were school books," Joey said. He walked backwards into the street, lifted the storm window. A car came at him and he ran most of the way up the hill, fell on his face, and slid down.

The car slowed down as it passed. "What's school?" I asked.

Joey stood in the mud. "A building where they make kids sit in chairs all day and don't let them pee." He pointed at his zipper. "If you pee your pants they pinch your hole shut with a clothespin."

I believed him. "Why do kids go there?"

"'Cause they aren't Indians."

"Why don't Indians go?"

"'Cause the authorities think we're on a reservation."

"But you're not on a reservation."

"So?"

"And I'm not Indian."

Joey closed his eyes to think that one over. "You should probably be in school then."

"Maybe the authorities don't know about me."

"Why wouldn't they?"

"Because my parents are dead."

Joey closed one eye. "I guess you're just lucky."

Another kid was walking down the sidewalk across the street, my color and bigger than Joey.

Joey put the storm window under his arm, cupped his hand. "FOOL, FOOL. YOU GOTS TO GO TO SCHOOL!"

The kid stopped and raised a fist. Joey grabbed at the muddy sidewalk, threw something in the kid's general direction.

The kid ran away.

"What you throw?" I asked.

He showed me his palms, walked backwards into the street. "Nothing."

A brown car came at him, beeping its horn. He faced it

and raised a fist. The car stopped. Used? I thought, and Joey ran at the hill, made it to the top, handed me the storm window. "Your turn."

The car drove off.

"What's the authorities?" I said.

"Cops. Firemen. Dads who aren't Indian."

"My dad wasn't Indian."

"But he's dead."

I knelt on the storm window, saw a car coming from a half block away. Joey pushed and I slid down the hill, across the muddy sidewalk and into the street—the car whizzing past me, blowing my hair to the side.

Then I stopped.

"YOU'RE LUCKY," Joey yelled, and he walked off.

I shovelled the sidewalk with my sore hand, spent the rest of the day in the neighbor's garage: hiding from the Indian Lady, Joey, and The Authorities.

Just before bedtime I found Diezee in the basement.

"Where's Fommy's room?" I asked her.

"Just walk through the front door, like you're company. His room used to be the living room."

As it turned out, the front door was the only way you could get to Fommy's room, because stacked boxes of canned damaged-in-shipment cling peaches covered the floor right up to the inside doorway. When I got in there that night, Fommy's mattress lay between the box stacks and a window, Fommy himself sitting on one of its corners in loose underwear. He saw me, tilted a peach can to his mouth, and hit it with the heel of his hand.

"Where'd your mom get these peaches?" I said.

"Train wreck auction." He held out the can. "Have some."

I ate half a peach, which chewed kind of dry. "No juice?"

"I drank it."

"You like it?"

"Not really."

"Then why drink it?"

He pointed to his mattress: pond-shaped yellow stains of various sizes, some with brown edges, one over the next. "I'm not 'posed to drink anything after supper. But then I get thirsty."

I ate another peach half, tilted the can, saw some juice. "Here."

Fommy took the can and guzzled. He held the can out at

me and I shook my head. He opened a window, threw out the can. It clanked on shovelled-clean sidewalk. He lay on the stains. "Could you please get the light?" he said.

I found and flipped off the switch. The light stayed on.

"You gotta unscrew it."

The boxes beneath the light were stacked like stairs. I climbed them and unscrewed the bulb with my sore hand, which hurt worse in the dark. I cleared my throat. "Where do I sleep?"

I heard Fommy move toward the window. A sewing room, a floor, and now this, I thought, then walked around a box stackand lay down. I heard breathing and smelled peach juice.

Beats dustballs and old toast, I thought. Then I began smelling the stains. My hand hurt worse, but not as bad as it did an hour later, when I woke to a strange hissing sound.

"Fommy?" I whispered.

"Yes?"

"Was that you?"

"Yes." I heard wet underwear hit the side of a box. "I'm sorry."

"That's okay," I told him.

But I won't, I told myself, sleep here again.

2

The Out

2,066 mornings later, I woke up. Fommy was sleeping against the wall. We were all bigger now: me, Fommy, the pee stains. The box stacks were shorter. I still wasn't in school. The front door opened—I was watching through quivering eyelids— and This-Here-Malcolm walked in, wearing pants. He wrung his hands like Ed Sullivan, took a box of canned peaches, and left.

I fell asleep, dreamt that the Indian Lady was tenderizing stew meat with a butcher knife, woke up to pounding on the door. Fommy crawled across the mattress in his underwear. They were loose but dry. That made three dry nights in a row. Maybe Fommy had it licked.

He moved three boxes and opened the door. A man with a face the color of raw pork sausage stood there in a uniform that wasn't the mailman's.

The Authorities, I thought, and I pulled the dry sheet over my head.

"Detective Lazewski," he said. "Malcolm here?"

"One moment," Fommy said. He turned to me. "Could you please wake up Malcolm?"

I covered my face with my hand, ran upstairs and climbed the rope ladder. The $21.99 squirrel monkey was sitting on the mattress with its arms crossed: no Malcolm.

I ran back downstairs. The Indian Lady was standing at the front door. She was bigger now, too. "He's up north," she told Detective Lazewski.

"Where up north."

"Near Tomah."

The Indian Lady slammed the door, grabbed a dented peach can, and left through the inside doorway. I heard her thighs rub: panty hose.

Then Fommy and I wrestled. I won. He was bored so we went to the kitchen, where the Indian Lady stood at the table ladling Farina into fifteen Salvation Army bowls.

"Again?" Fommy said.

She held the ladle as if she were ready to serve his ear over a badminton net. "Farina or you starve."

Fommy ate Farina. I ate mine with a measuring spoon: six and a half tablespoons of Farina. The Indian Lady slurped peach halves from the dented can, cutting coupons from the *Sentinel* with used pinking shears. The other Indian kids appeared one by one, barefoot. They all ate Farina.

The Indian Lady chewed her last peach half, then picked up and waved her new coupons. "No one leaves while I'm gone," she said with someone else's voice—the peach was halfway down her throat—and left through the back door.

Joey sat sipping the peach syrup from her damaged can. He pointed at me. "You and Diezee do the dishes."

"Me?" Diezee said.

Joey took aim and threw. The can hit the wall an inch beside Diezee's head. He picked his teeth with a fingernail. "Next time I'll aim."

Diezee set the Salvation Army bowls and spoons on the trampled-hard dirt of the backyard. I went in the basement and turned on the hose. She sprayed the dishes. The sun dried them.

We brought them back in the house, where the Indian kids were putting their shoes on.

"Where you goin'?" Diezee said.

"Clubbing."

Clubbing meant going to Pulaski Park, pouring coffee cans of lagoon water into gopher holes, and clubbing scared gophers with whiffle bats until their mouths bled.

"No clubbing for me," I told Joey. I was twelve years old and growing bolder all the time.

"Says who," Joey said.

"Your ma."

"Fine. But tell on us and you're dead."

The Indian kids left. I climbed into This-Here-Malcolm's room, to catch the squirrel monkey.

The mattress was nothing but pillows. The sunflower seed bowl was half empty. I grabbed a handful of seeds and began throwing them one by one at the rafters.

I threw thirty-six seeds and heard a voice:

"Where's everyone else?"

This-Here-Malcolm's sunglasses were peering over the trapdoor. His forehead was white and sweating.

I threw a seed. "Clubbing. Except your ma. She's shopping."

This-Here-Malcolm heaved himself onto the floor, watched me throw seeds.

"Anyone . . . stop by this morning?" he asked. His spine was curved like a dry leaf's, his doughy stomach divided like sliced bread.

"Yeah," I said. "A guy named Lazewski. A detective."

"Oh."

I threw seeds: thirty-eight, thirty-nine, forty.

"Hunting buddy of mine," This-Here Malcolm said. "You wanna go hunting?"

"For what."

"Anything. I'm moving up north to run a business. On a reservation. You hunt whatever you want whenever you want. Deer, rabbit, squirrel, possum . . . *anything.*"

Forty-one. "What kinda business?" Forty-two, forty-three, forty-four—

"A trout hatchery."

This-Here-Malcolm's lies reminded me of Norb Hike's. "What's a trout hatchery?"

"Man-made stream you raise fish in. You feed the fish corn till they're fat, then starve them. Families from Chicago in station wagons pay good money to catch them." He lifted his glasses off his nose and pinned me down with his rosary bead eyes. "I could use a helper."

Forty-five, forty-six, forty-seven.

"Someone to skin 'em," he said.

Forty-eight, forty-nine.

"The trout, I mean." He dropped his sunglasses back on his nose. "There's also some used cars up there we could fix and sell."

Used cars? I thought.

Fifty.

"I'm leaving tonight," he said. "But you can't tell anyone."

"Why not?"

He had to think that one over. "'Cause if Ma knew, she wouldn't let you go."

Used cars, I thought. "I'm in."

"Good man. When everyone comes back, you act like it's

just another day. Tonight you stay awake and listen for a knock on the door. I'll have the car running."

"I didn't know you had a car."

This-Here-Malcolm raised his glasses off his nose. "I'll have one tonight."

I heard cabinet doors slam in the kitchen. "Your ma's home."

"Go downstairs and act like it's just another day."

I went downstairs, walked into the kitchen. The Indian Lady and the Indian kids were there, eating banana sandwiches.

I ate a banana sandwich as if it were just another day.

The Indian Lady ate three banana sandwiches as if there were no tomorrow.

Then she went to the bathroom.

Joey stood on a chair, stared at me as if we knew something no one else did. "We're all going goldfish hunting," he said, and the Indian kids clapped and whistled. Diezee ran into the girl's bedroom, came back with a butterfly net, which Fommy kept trying to grab. Joey took a milk carton out of the refrigerator, emptied it into the sink. We finished our banana sandwiches, walked to Mitchell Street, hid behind a dumpster near a Chinese restaurant beside a small concrete pond.

Joey grabbed the butterfly net from Fommy. "Watch for Art."

"Art?" I said.

"Art Woijokowski," Fommy whispered. "He owns the Chinese restaurant. Just watch the backdoor."

Joey snuck up to the concrete pond and lifted the butterfly net above his head. The backdoor opened. A man in a bloody T-shirt ran out waving a fry-pan.

"*ZATRZYMAJ SIE BRZYDKI* KIDS!"

We ran.

"*ZATRZYMAJ SIE!*"

The Hand

The mattress was dry. I rolled off it, sat on a box of damaged-in-shipment canned peaches, heard nothing but Fommy breathing. Good boy, I thought. Then I heard the little knock. I opened the door. This-Here-Malcolm stood on the porch wearing sunglasses. His pants were black and shiny, his hair combed like licorice whips. A '54 Studebaker sat on the street coughing white puffs of exhaust.

"Ready?"

I look at Fommy, the boxes, the pee stains. "Yeah."

This-Here-Malcolm led me to the Studebaker. I got in on the passenger side. The engine almost choked, and there was something cold and furry beside me.

"What's this?" I said, pointing.

This-Here-Malcolm switched on the domelight. Mangled in a rat trap the size of a shoe box cover was the $21.99 squirrel monkey. Blood covered the corners of its mouth like dried ketchup on carnival garbage.

"Finally got the little bastard," This-Here-Malcolm said. He grabbed the steering wheel, shifted into first. "Used a squirrel trap." We knifed ahead. "Thought you'd wanna see him."

The windshield whistled. A shiver grabbed my shoulders.

"Squirrel trap for a squirrel monkey," I said. I stared straight ahead until I noticed the headlights weren't on.

Then This-Here-Malcolm turned off the domelight. All I could see was the shine of his licorice whip hair.

"You know your headlights aren't on?"

He kept driving.

"I know," he finally said, and he hit the brakes. We skidded and stopped. He rolled down his window, yanked the squirrel monkey from the squirrel trap, threw it out the window. It landed on the street four car lengths in front of us: eleven o'clock high.

"Watch," he said. The brights went on and we inched ahead. The left beam covered the monkey. This-Here-Malcolm revved the engine. His eyes rolled like marbles in wind and we screeched ahead.

Driving over a dead monkey feels like stepping on a bruised crabapple.

He turned off the highbeams and sped on.

"Well?" he said.

"Well what."

"Pretty keen, hey?"

"Sure."

We sped for blocks, not talking.

Then This-Here-Malcolm said, "Just one stop before we head up north. Gotta get something from a buddy of mine's garage."

"What's that."

We kept speeding.

"Something from his garage."

I began missing Fommy. This-Here-Malcolm took four turns. The last went into an alley, a hill at least a block long. He cut the engine and we rolled to the bottom and stopped beside a garage. Somewhere, someone's dog barked.

This-Here-Malcolm took a key off the dashboard, got out of the Studebaker and unlocked the garage door, a heavy wooden one. He lifted it and walked inside. All I could see was his T-shirt moving around like a ghost. I began counting, to pass time.

At eighty-six he began dragging a box toward the Studebaker. "Wanna help?"

I got out, grabbed an end, smelled rotten lawn clippings.

"Careful," he said.

"Sure is heavy."

We slid the box to the rear end of the Studebaker. He opened the trunk.

"That smell coming from the box?" I asked.

"What smell."

"That rotting smell. Like lawn clippings." I put my nose to a box corner. "It *is* from here. You sure you got the right box?"

"Sure I'm sure." He started lifting. "There's a . . . pool liner in here. My buddy's lending it to me so we can put a pool on the reservation. One of those above-ground deals. Must be a little mold on it." He nodded at my end of the box and lifted his end. I lifted mine. The box was halfway to the trunk when the bottom fell through, the pool liner slapping the alley a good one.

Only it didn't look like a pool liner.

It looked like a used plastic drop-cloth spattered with red paint.

This-Here-Malcolm covered it with the box. "Looks a little dirty. My buddy musta painted some lawn furniture near it. Look outta here—I'll get it myself." He wrapped his arm around the box and lifted it onto his thigh. Something fell from the bottom to the alley.

"Dropped one of your buddy's painting gloves," I said, and I picked up the thing.

Only the thing wasn't a glove. It was a hand, a human hand I was holding as if I were being introduced to someone. I looked closer: it was black.

I'd never touched a black man before and now I was shaking one's hand and the rest of him wasn't attached.

The rest of him was dead, in the drop cloth, smelling like rotten grass clippings.

"Oh boy," I said.

There wasn't enough air in the alley. This-Here-Malcolm looked at the hand. He lifted his sunglasses onto his head and smiled. "Must have taken the wrong box," he said. He grabbed the hand, held it in front of his face like a pawnbroker. It stunk bad—and got worse. He flipped it as if it were a coin, catching it in his palm. "Pretty neat, huh?"

I couldn't breathe. I sat on the damp alley. He slid the hand into his back pocket fingers first and grabbed my live white one. Then he pulled. I was standing now, shaky. He squeezed my hand, wouldn't let go, opened the cardboard box with his free hand. All the hands were making me dizzy. He grabbed a knife, a big kitchen one. The blade flashed in the moonlight and my head spun. He squeezed my fingers, pressed the blade against my wrist and began sawing. My skin wouldn't cut: the knife was that dull. "Dammit," he said, and he sawed, and I yanked my hand away—from him—and took off. Garages flew past me. I couldn't breathe. I almost fell twice. The Studebaker roared into ignition, its high beams on me. I pictured the squirrel monkey, ran faster, then cut to the right, between garages.

Something hard grabbed my face: a chain link fence. A king-size poodle stood behind it, barking. "Nice doggie," I said.

It was the color of apricots, huge, and barked as if volume made dog biscuits. I climbed the fence, fell onto the dog's back, grabbed what I could of its tail. It yelped and sprinted across the yard, dragging me over dewy, slick grass. I looked over my shoulder, saw This-Here-Malcolm climbing the fence with the knife between his teeth, squeezed the dog's tail. It ran faster, barking and yelping through a hedgerow, down a hill, up a street, over more front and back yards. Black windows turned yellow. 3Ps opened doors. The tail slipped from my hand and the poodle ran off—down a long street.

I looked over my shoulder, to my left, to my right: no sign of Malcolm. Then I saw headlights, behind me, growing brighter. Red lights began flashing. The Authorities! I thought, and a police car screeched behind me.

I ran left.

"Come back here, hey!"

I ran so fast I was falling. Bungalows blurred past me until I came to a wide street with signs: National Avenue. I stopped and looked around. No one was behind me. No one was anywhere. Downtown Milwaukee—tiny lights that winked—lay an odometer mile in front of me. I was, I realized, on the edge of 3P territory. My wrist hurt but was barely bleeding.

I began catching my breath. I was alone. I was alive. There was nothing but me, National Avenue, and those tiny winking lights.

The Reading Room

I'd spent two days in the Industrial Valley, a playground of coal piles, salt piles, railroad cars and curves of green river. Now I was downtown and hungry, across a busy street from a building covered with pigeon droppings. People were walking in and out using the thick glass doors, people of all kinds.

Then: some kids walked in with mothers and fathers. I crossed the street, went in where they did.

There were books everywhere, and a counter without a cash register. A man and a woman stood behind the counter. They both looked hungrier than I was, both had hair the color of boxcar rats. Their foreheads were shiny. Maybe they, I thought, were my mother and father.

I walked up to the counter.

"I hate them," the woman said.

"So messy," the man said.

Then they saw me and pretended they'd never met each other.

"You talking about kids?" I said.

The woman smiled at the man. "No. Pigeons."

"I like kids," the man said. He sounded more like a woman than the woman did.

"Is there something you wanted to learn about?" she asked me.

I looked out the thick glass doors. A car drove by, looking used. "Cars," I said. "Used ones."

"My turn," the woman told the man. She pushed through a little door that looked like part of the counter. "Follow me," she said, and I did.

She walked quickly on worn soles the color of dried yellow glue. Then she ran her finger across the backs of shelved books, some thicker than others, most red, blue or green.

"These are all about used cars," she said. "Was there something specific you wanted to read about?" She wiped a string of rat-colored hair across her shiny forehead and smiled. Her shoulders looked disconnected.

"No."

She kept smiling.

"You ever sell used cars?" I asked.

"I've been a librarian ever since high school."

"That's nice," I said.

She turned, began walking away, and stopped. She looked over her shoulder. "You know where the reading room is?"

I shook my head.

She pointed down the aisle, at a wooden door. A white-haired man in a blue sport coat stood beside it. "You can read in there all day," she said, "as long as you have a book."

I took a book off the shelf—*Shade Tree Mechanic: Removing Six and Eight Cylinder Engines*—and walked down the aisle. The man in the blue coat had pink ears and a hearing aid the color of crutch tops. The look on his cross-eyed face spoke for him:

You got a book?
You ain't a pigeon?
Enjoy your reading.

I walked in: more green tile, avocado-colored chairs against the walls, old men sitting in torn clothes and smashed fedoras missing feathers. They looked at me: red eyes, purple noses, yellow teeth. One scratched his chin. Three needed shaves. All ignored pigeons.

The pigeons were pacing the concrete sills outside the windows, pecking the thick glass, shrugging their shoulders. I sat in an avocado chair, glanced at *Shade Tree Mechanic*. The Reading Room Men watched me but never said a word. Then they began closing their eyes.

But they all had books.

And they weren't pigeons.

I looked at pictures of bad spark plugs in *Shade Tree Mechanic*, ignoring pigeons like the rest of the guys.

Suddenly the door opened—and a round-faced man walked in.

He had a book in his hand.

He wasn't a pigeon.

He was Norb Hike.

His pass to the reading room was the 1964 *Bluebook of Wholesale and Retail Car Prices*. He sat in an avocado chair, then craned his neck to look at the pigeons.

One of the Reading Room Men opened an eye, shut it immediately. He'd seen Norb Hike looking at pigeons, and he'd seen enough.

Pig nose wrinkled, Norb Hike looked around. His eyes met mine and blinked hard. His head, which had less hair on it than the last time I'd seen it, motioned me over to him.

Even his head talks, I thought. This man is my hero. I nodded and walked over.

"See them pigeons out there?" he said.

I glanced at the Reading Room Men, not wanting them to see me see pigeons. Their eyes were all closed. My left armpit was moist as the sponge my grandmother had tied to the tub faucet to save water. I peeked out the window. The pigeons were dusty black, like stones beneath railroad tracks.

"Suckers are worth cash," Norb Hike said.

I looked at his small ears, disappointed that he didn't recognize me, excited about turning pigeons into money.

"Not all of 'em," he said. "Just the ones with the feathers all the way down their legs. See that brown one with feathers all the way down his legs?"

I looked at the Reading Room Men. They were still sleeping. I glanced at the only brown pigeon on the window sill. Its legs had feathers all the way down them.

Norb Hike loosened his belt a notch. "Not at all like your standard scaly red pigeon leg."

"Sonofagun," I said. My right armpit was moist: things were coming together nicely.

"Guy at the Seven Mile Fair'll pay two bucks for that pigeon," Norb Hike said. "You know what I'm talking about, the Seven Mile Fair?"

I nodded three times. Norb Hike not recognizing me didn't matter anymore. We were talking money.

"And if it's got—sonofa*buck*, that one's got the tuft on the head. You see that tuft on its head?"

I looked out the window. The brown pigeon had a tuft on its head.

"Yeah."

"That's three more dollars right there."

I looked at Norb Hike's smile, felt the corners of my lips

try to lift themselves. "*Five* dollars for a stupid pigeon?"

"You darn right," he said. His pig nose moved up and down: confusing.

"How do you catch them?"

A Reading Room Man lifted his head and screwed his index finger knuckles into his eye sockets, elbows raised, arms fanned out like wings, legs tan but without feathers.

"That's where you come in," Norb Hike said. His smile disappeared. "Hang on a second. I gotta price a car."

"A used one?"

He nodded and paged through the *Blue Book*. A shiver zipped down my spine. He paged forward, backward, forward. I fixed my eyes on the thick lips under his pig-nose: maybe he'd explain a used car man's secret.

"Darned alphabet," he said.

He flipped a page and put his finger on a column of numbers. His finger was stubby and stained with dirty motor oil and moved slowly down the column. Its nail was chewed down to three-eighths of an inch, if it was lucky.

Then the fingertip stopped, nail white, then pink, then red.

"Six-fifty," he said.

"*Six-fifty*," my lips said without voice.

He took a complimentary Kosciusko Savings and Loan pen from behind his ear and wrote on the back of his hand:

Offer $150—TOPS.

In minutes I was standing on a shady sidewalk outside the building holding a landing net close to my heart. Sixty-four bread crumbs were scattered around me.

"The only secret," Norb Hike said. He took two little tubes out of his pocket. "Is that seven crumbs should be epoxied to the sidewalk exactly two feet in front of you." He began gluing crumbs to the sidewalk.

I cleared my throat. "Is this legal?"

"If a cop asks what you're doing, say you're catching a pet homer that got lost in a thunderstorm. Whereas if *I'm* standing there, he'd have me thrown in the rubber room simple as whistlin' Dixie."

Then he said something I'll never forget:

"It's all how you present yourself, kid."

He smiled. His lips were worm red, and kept smiling. His eyes moved down my face without either of us talking, and then, for the first time ever, it happened: my straight lips tightened and rose at the corners.

"I like that smile," he said, and he slapped my back.

Feeling wind against my teeth, I kept smiling.

He finished gluing crumbs, got in his used car, and took off.

I didn't.

I stood on that shady sidewalk holding a net for three and a half hours, smiling.

Finally a pigeon swooped down and landed seventeen feet away from me. It circled me three times, bobbing its head and watching me out of the corner of its eye, then pecked at a crumb and darted away.

Suddenly the sky was full of squeaking. Pigeons were landing on the sidewalk like fighter planes, pecking the loose crumbs and each other, closing in on me, the epoxied crumbs, and the landing net. I smiled harder and thought: Today, pigeons. Tomorrow, used cars.

Then the sidewalk was pure pigeon. When a white one with black feathers on it legs began pecking an epoxied bread crumb, I dropped the landing net, 136 pigeons flapping, squeaking and rising—and messing my hair with wing wind and gray shit.

But it was worth it.

I'd caught a pigeon worth cash money.

Now all I had to do was put it in the used cardboard box hidden in shrubbery on the boulevard, catch nine more, and get the box to the Seven Mile Fair by seven next morning, a Sunday.

Joan's Bones

The Seven Mile Fair hadn't changed since the days I'd sold Mickey Mouse balloons for my dead grandfather.

There were still hundreds of round-faced 3Ps there, sitting on rainsoaked armchairs and milk crates in their leased wooden shacks and selling basement junk: used steel-toed boots, used plastic silverware, used prayer books, used accordions, used *Playboy* magazines, and other bargain necessities.

The 3P children still stood near their parents' shacks, sweating, shooing jumbo horseflies, making sure no one swiped or broke anything. The whitewashed shack still sold redhots, roasted corn-on-the-cob, and fountain Pepsi-Cola with little flavor syrup and no bubbles, sucking away every penny of 3P profit.

I went straight to my dead grandfather's shack. Used Pepsi-Cola cups containing chocolate-colored soil were lined on the dirt floor like theater seats. Norb Hike stood beside them holding a cup, talking to a 3P fisherman.

"How much?" the fisherman said. He held a used Zebco in his left hand reel-end down, his walking stick to fishing heaven.

Norb Hike saw my cardboard box, then nodded. "Stand back and watch," the nod said. "I'm ready to make a sale."

I stood back and watched.

"Buck and a quarter for the dozen," Norb Hike said, looking off into space. A piece of roasted corn sat on the corner of his mouth, which the fisherman watched.

"Ten bits for twelve stinkin' worms?"

"These here are *nightcrawlers*," Norb Hike said. He tilted the used Pepsi-Cola cup to his face as if preparing to gulp down the soil. "Six to eight inches long, on the average. Break 'em in thirds and they'll still squirm on a hook for three-four hours. Thirty-six dancing redworms for a buck and a quarter is what your gettin' here. That's what—two, three cents a worm? You can't find a two cent redworm *anywhere*. And these'll keep in your icebox. Six months minimum. Take it or leave it. I got another customer here wanting to buy a boxfull."

The fisherman looked at me.

Norb Hike winked.

I set the box down at his feet, hoping the pigeons would keep their mouths shut. "I'll take a gross," I said. "For today."

"Not before I do," the fisherman said. "I was here first."

"The man has a point there, son," Norb Hike said. "You'll have to take what's left over." He turned to the fisherman. "How many?"

"Two gross," the fisherman said.

Norb Hike began counting Pepsi-Cola cups. The cardboard box began quivering. I picked it up and began walking away. "I'll be back," I said. "I need to use the Port-a-John."

I walked once around the Seven Mile Fair, stopping near a cracked ten gallon fish tank full of used buttons. None of the buttons matched but you could buy three for a penny. A sweating humpbacked 3P woman sifted a handful through her fingers, squinting:

If I could just find a red leather one . . . like the one . . . Edward lost bowling yesterday . . .

A policeman walked by and looked at me. I smiled like Norb Hike would, and the policeman nodded.

I returned to the shack. Norb Hike stood in front of it with his Jack-O-Lantern grin and his arms folded, raising and lowering his heels. The Pepsi-Cola cups were gone.

"I owe you a redhot," he said.

Joan Hike walked out from the back room—where my dead grandfather had kept his illegal sparklers—peeling used wax paper off something on her palm.

Every speck of that wax paper was wrinkled. She held out her palm. "Neck bone?"

"Sure," Norb Hike said.

There were two neck bones. Norb Hike looked them over. Joan Hike swept the dirt floor with her eyes. "Sold out?"

Norb Hike took the bigger neckbone and nodded. His grinning teeth tore themselves a mouthful of dry meat and skin. He breathed through his pig nose while he chewed, pointing the neckbone at me. "Couldn't have done it without my helper here."

Joan Hike saw me. "That's Sophie's grandson."

I froze like a robin listening for breakfast.

"Sonofa*buck* if it isn't," Norb Hike said, still chewing. He held the neckbone seven inches from his shoulder, tapped the air like a Polka band drummer. "Stretched out about two-three inches, but Sophie's grandson through and through. You remember us, kid?"

Of course I remembered the Hikes, right down to their bankrupt corner hardware store house and singing daughter, Pam Hike.

Answer like a used car salesman, I thought. "Remember you from where."

"We were friends of your grandparents," Joan Hike said.

I knew one reason I shouldn't admit remembering the Hikes: they'd return me to the Indian Lady's house, where This-Here-Malcolm would saw off my hands and maybe strangle me with a used extension cord.

"You were?" I asked Joan Hike.

"Of course."

I had no choice but to try to out-talk the best talker I'd ever met, Norb Hike, and his wife, Joan Hike. "You lived in California?"

"What's this with California?" Joan Hike said.

I looked at her as if California were written in crayon on my forehead. "I'm *from* California."

Grooves appeared between her eyebrows. "Where in California."

"The east part."

The grooves deepened. Norb Hike's bald head was cocked. He grinned at me, holding the neckbone next to his shoulder. "Maybe it ain't Sophie's grandkid."

Joan Hike cocked her head in the same direction as his. "You think?" Her open palm supported the wrinkled wax paper and smaller neckbone like a plant stand. A horsefly landed on her neckbone—the one she was eating.

"Sophie's grandkid never said a word," Norb Hike said.

They stood looking at me with their heads cocked side by side. The horsefly hopped onto Joan Hike's hair. Norb Hike winked at me. "Whereas this-here kid's a *talker*."

When Joan Hike looked at her feet, I winked back.

Wheeling and Dealing

The Indian reservation excuse was out the window.

The Authorities were hot on my trail.

So it was do whatever Norb Hike and Liquid Johnny said or go to grade school.

For a hundred nightcrawlers a day I could also eat leftover donuts and sleep in Liquid Yoshu's Sparkling Motors' toolcrib.

Liquid Yoshu's Sparkling Motors was Liquid Johnny's used car lot. At one time it had been "Liquid Johnny's Sparkling Motors," but Liquid Johnny had learned "Yoshu" was Polish for "Johnny" and changed the name.

I did whatever they said there.

The nightcrawler deal was a little trickier: there had to be exactly a hundred nightcrawlers, and they had to be *nightcrawlers*. Worms didn't count. Half-nightcrawlers didn't, either.

According to Norb Hike, half-nightcrawlers oozed a pus that could wipe out a worm farm like polio. That scared me.

Norb Hike gave me a few tips before my first night's hunting. We were standing on Liquid Yoshu's lot, among thirty-nine used cars. Strung lightbulbs made it hard to see. I was happy.

"Most worm men believe your nightcrawler won't show unless it's drowning, like say during a rain storm. That theory's only part right. It's *panic* that brings 'em up. So instead of waiting for a storm, you pound a two-by-four about three foot into the ground. I've brought up five-six hundred crawlers at a time that way."

"Is that right?" I said.

He picked his nose with his pinky. "The things are thinking earthquake."

Minutes later I stood in Pulaski Park with a flashlight tied to the top of my head, pounding the end of a two-by-four with a chunk of asphalt. Three feet is a long way for a two-by-four.

Mine only went three inches. No nightcrawlers appeared.

I jumped up and down 437 times: still no nightcrawlers.

My feet hurt so I pounded 217 more times. The two-by-four was six inches deep. The worms weren't panicking, but I was.

What would a used car man do? I wondered. I began walking to Norb Hike's house, to talk. Don't let Joan Hike see you, I thought, and I noticed a small 3P lawn with a back-and-forth sprinkler going.

Drowning, I thought. I adjusted my flashlight and began hunting. Nightcrawler tips glistened like saliva. I caught some, missed some, then heard an old 3P voice from behind the screen door:

"I goddit da gun on you, butch. One step closer an I shootchoo so full a holes you won't know which you gonna shit from."

I turned off my flashlight, looked up and saw a tiny orange dot: the glowing end of a cigarette, probably a Salem.

3Ps enjoyed their Salems.

"Sorry, sir," I said. "Just hunting nightcrawlers."

The orange dot moved up and down: "Not *here* you no hunttit da crawlers."

Something clinked just below the dot, probably dogtags on a weiner dog scratching its neck with its hind leg.

3Ps loved their weiner dogs.

"I just chrow bluegrass seet dat cost a buck sixty-nine plus salessstax. Now geddit da hell out."

"I'm sorry, sir."

"Don't sorry me. Just geddit da hell out."

"I'm leaving right now, sir."

"You come back ever, I call it da cops."

I walked half a block away and hid behind an elm tree. The orange dot disappeared, the door creaked closed, and the lights in the house went out, the orange dot moving from window to window. When it disappeared for good I counted to a thousand. Then I snuck up to the last window I'd seen it in and flicked on my flashlight. The old 3P was curled like a kitten on a pile of laundry, eyes closed, mouth open, a weiner dog asleep on the side of his head.

I got my hundred nightcrawlers.

I took them to the scorched Quonset hut Norb Hike had bought at an arson auction and kept behind his bankrupt hardware store house: part of the deal. I put the nightcrawlers in a steel bucket of water in a used Frigidaire there.

Cold water relaxed worms, according to The Panic Theory.

Then I walked the six blocks to Liquid Yoshu's Sparkling Motors. I opened its garage door with the only key I'd ever touched in my life and lay on a pile of oily rags. The cleanest rag covered a used muffler: a hungry used car man's pillow.

Kasha

Something smelled like baked chicken. I lay there, in the tool crib. A man as wide as a truck tire stepped onto the used bathroom scale beneath the postage-stamp-red wallphone, then stretched his neck so he could see beneath his waist.

"Three hundred poundos," he said.

Then he took half an engine out of a car, Bondoed a rear quarter panel, taped some ripped upholstery from the inside of a back seat . . .

I sat up and watched.

. . . patched a flat tire, fixed an automatic transmission by putting a penny in it, poured used cooking oil in a crank case, and stepped on the scale again, sweating like Orson Welles in a sauna.

"*Still* three hundred."

He walked in the tool crib as if I weren't there and sat on a stool. The stool disappeared but the baked chicken smell got stronger.

"Hike says you're a natural," he said, pronouncing his s's like a leaking tire nozzle. His shirt introduced him: GARY. Tire-colored rings surrounded his wet gray eyes. Tiny cloth-balls covered the thighs of his blue pants. His white socks sagged enough that I could see his fat shins: powdered milk white, only a few hairs.

"Natural what," I said.

"Talker."

"Mr. Hike told you that?"

"I can't figure it out either. You haven't said jack all morning."

"I didn't know I was supposed to."

"*Supposed* to? Since when does supposed to matter in this business?"

I'm learning already, I thought. "Since I don't wanna bug anyone."

He popped a donut in his mouth: one less for my supper. "Don't wanna bug anyone," he said, chewing. He licked the face of his thumb, yanked one of his socks from between his shoe and ankle. I could still see his white shin, just not as much of it. "You know anything about selling used cars?"

"I know there's money in it."

Powdered sugar flew from his mouth: "How you know that?"

"My grandfather."

"He sell cars?"

"He bought a few."

"Someone take him pretty bad?"

I nodded. "Mr. Hike."

"Call him Norb. Hey, wait a second. And now you're pickin' nightcrawlers for him? I don't follow."

"You would if you knew my grandfather."

"You don't like your grandfather?"

"*Didn't.* He's dead."

Gary closed an eye, as if having two open prevented thinking. "Ain't he the one that busted his head at Honey Helen's . . . how shall we say, *sugar* shop?"

I nodded. "Started out with electrical problems."

"Oldest scam in the book."

"You mean there's more?"

Gary slid another donut in his mouth: two less for supper. "*Shit*chyeah. I could talk scams till your balls drop." He glanced at the timeclock, pointed at a five gallon paint can cornered by two pegboard walls. "Take a look in there."

I walked over to the paint can. There was an old alternator on the lid.

"Throw that on the floor."

I threw the alternator on the floor, opened the can, stood looking at four and a half gallons of pennies, nickels, dimes, quarters, fifty cent pieces—even a few silver dollars.

"Wow."

"You know where that came from?"

I shook my head.

"Everytime some asshole trades in a car, we check behind the seats. You just shove your hand in there—in that ass crack where the seat belts get lost?—and you're guaranteed a couple bucks. Of course you'll come up with a lot of trash, too—combs, hair pins, church bulletins."

Another donut: three.

"But you'll always come up with money. And we don't just check trade-ins, either. We check the cars the assholes leave here while they test-drive ours. Guy comes back and says he don't want the car? Fine with us. We've already taken him."

A doorbell buzzed. Gary stood up. The stool surprised me: it was there. He grabbed two donuts—that made five—and stuffed them in his mouth and walked to a garage door window. Chewing, he stared out for a long time. "So long, sucker." He walked over to the scale, stepped on it, and threw up his hands. "Three *fucking* hundred."

I shrugged.

"Wanna get this one?" he asked.

"Huh?"

"Some skinny broad is out test-driving with Johnny. Her Buick's right outside the door. Wanna check the seats?"

"Sure."

He lifted the garage door, led me outside. A fat yellow Buick sat between two painted-over runners. He got on his hands and knees, punched at something near the right rear tire with a screwdriver, raised an eyebrow in my direction. "Hole in the muffler. Makes 'em wanna sell. Easy to fix." He began walking toward the garage. "Go ahead with the seats."

I got in on the driver's side, slid my hand behind the cushion, felt something cool and round, pulled it out: a quarter. I tried again. Two nickels and a penny. Then a glove, some tangled hair, a fifty cent piece. More hair. Then something crumpled . . . a dollar bill!

I thought: Till my *balls* drop.

I looked out the window. The garage door was shut. My thighs tingled more than my hands trembled. I crammed the money into my pocket, dove into the back seat: a wire hanger, three dimes, two pennies. Then something that felt like another bill—but stuck there. Like the gold specks on my grandmother's bathroom floor, I thought, and I pulled carefully. Whatever it was wouldn't come. I pulled at different angles, used my other hand. Finally it slid free:

TEN DOLLARS.

"Shitchyeah," I whispered. I heard a voice: Liquid Johnny's, getting louder. I looked out the back window. A woman and Liquid stood talking. She turned and I ducked, put the ten in my pocket, and listened to myself breathe. The driver's door opened and closed. I lay on the floor, facing a rust hole. The car started and the engine roared.

"Oh, God," the woman's voice said. She put it in gear, accelerated. The roar got louder. I watched concrete move past the rust hole.

"Demons be gone," she said, and the roar got louder still. The concrete moved faster until black smoke poured through the hole. I closed my mouth, held my breath until I couldn't. Then I breathed through my nose and again held my breath. The roar made my head spin. My eyes kept trying to close.

"DEMONS BE GONE!" the woman shouted.

Then I was someplace else, still lying down but flipped over like a half-done hamburger, still smelling smoke but not the black stuff, and not baked chicken, either. A bedsheet covered me, up to my mouth. I breathed in the smell: used cigarette smoke. The pillow under my head smelled the same way. A plastic chandelier hung from the ceiling with six dusty yellow light bulbs shaped like flames. Two worked. On a card table to my right sat a fish tank: six flat silver fish sucking dollar-green water. Bubbles rose from a pink shell like inflated coins. Orange gravel glowed. Beside the tank sat an ashtray containing fourteen smashed cigarette butts, most pink from lipstick.

I looked to my left. Statues crowded the floor: a two-foot plastic Virgin Mary, a tiny ceramic Joseph, St. John, St. Paul, St. Cosmas, St. Damian—all the saints. Jesus was there, too, thirteen Jesuses of different ages and sizes. The giant baby one lying in a popsicle stick manger looked at me with tiny men's eyes.

Click: something beyond the foot of my bed. I looked. A flame licked a cigarette between a woman's painted-red lips. The lips made me nervous but the eyes looked familiar. She wore a red cape, was skinny, sat on a purple hassock, had a gold blanket over her legs. Smoke shot from her nostrils, the only wide thing about her. The rest of her was hidden under her cape and blanket, looking ready to break.

Click: the flame disappeared. She set a lighter shaped like a Christmas elf on a small hassock beside her—I could barely see it in the dull yellow light.

She lifted her chin. "My baby Jesus brought you back."

The blanket glittered. She took the cigarette from her mouth, twisted it between her thumb and finger as if it were a dial on a dashboard radio.

I'd never seen a woman smoke before. "Who are you?"

"Kasha the Healer. I found you in my back seat. You were dead for twelve hours. My baby Jesus brought you back." She hung her cigarette on her lower lip, grabbed a used holy water sprinkler, waved it at me like a fisherman. A cool drop hit my forehead. She smiled. "You owe me ten dollars."

Ten dollars, I thought. My hands went to my pockets: no pants.

"I washed them," she said. "Clean of the demons. Your money's under your pillow."

I sat up, lifted the pillow. The coins and dollar bill were there. The ten wasn't. I looked at the saints, the Christmas elf lighter, then her. "You owe *me* ten dollars."

She smiled. "For what?"

"For stealing it. I had ten more dollars in my pocket. It's gone."

"You know where it went?" The gold blanket slid off her legs. They were crossed, looked tangled: skinnier than I'd thought, worse than crows' legs. She uncrossed them slowly until the red cape covered the top halves of her thighs.

"No."

"*I* do." She gapped her kneecaps four inches. "Wanna guess where?"

"Your purse?"

"Wrong." Her knees spread six inches, seven inches. The cape slid higher. Her thighs were thin as banisters but I didn't want to grab them.

Twelve inches.

I saw my ten dollars, folded like a tent in the orange shade of the cape.

"You see what you want?"

"Yeah."

"You still want it?"

I coughed: new cigarette smoke. "Sure."

"Come get it."

"I'm not wearing pants."

"Get over here or you won't see those either."

I got out of the bed in my shirt and underwear: hers. It was tight—she was that skinny. I started walking, toward her but slowly.

Her thighs clapped closed. "On your knees."

I looked at the saints. A short prayer for ten dollars, I

thought, so I knelt, facing the fish tank.

She leaned back against the wall, gapped her knees eighteen inches. "Crawl to mommy."

"I don't have a mommy."

"*I'm* your mommy."

"You can't be. She's dead."

"You want your ten bucks, kid?"

I nodded.

"*Crawl.*"

I crawled onto an oval rug crocheted from used nylons and scarves. "That's enough crawling. Give me my ten."

The doorbell rang, kept ringing.

"God *darn* it. WHO'S THERE?"

"Me," a voice said—my grandmother's. "Sophie. For healing, I'm here. I just cashed my Social Security."

Kasha pulled the cape over her knees, stood with her thighs together, walked to the door with the ten dollars between them: tiny steps. I crawled to the bed, tried to hide among the saints. Their eyes looked sad and angry. Some of their heads were bleeding.

Kasha opened the door and my grandmother pushed in, fanning herself with a handful of dollar bills. Her nose had grown since the last time I'd seen her. Kasha backed up, her eyes on the bills. My ten dollars fell from her legs, landed on the floor past the saints. My grandmother stepped on it, sat on the small hassock, knocked the Christmas elf lighter to the floor. She looked at the ceiling as if it were God. "What's that knocking up there?"

Kasha kept looking at the bills. "Spirits."

My grandmother made the sign of the cross. I looked under the bed. Something with legs lay there: my pants. I grabbed them, began putting them on.

"Just the healing this time," my grandmother told Kasha. "But double strength. My corns hurt like pin cushions, I have the ringing in the ear, my shoulder is numb . . ."

Kasha sat on the big hassock. "What your chiropractor ask?"

"Fifteen dollars with no guarantee. My neck is stiff, I got the swollen gland again . . ."

"I'll guarantee for twelve."

My grandmother took off her bifocals, began rubbing her eyes.

I crawled and grabbed my ten dollars, then stood and walked toward the door.

"For God's *sake*," my grandmother said.

I walked out, closed the door behind me.

"FOR GOD'S SAKE I SAW THE BOY JESUS!"

Sharks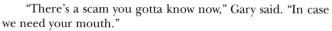

"There's a scam you gotta know now," Gary said. "In case we need your mouth."

I sat up on my tool box handle, with my best posture. I was wearing my own underwear.

"All you gotta remember is: 'My ma wants to buy. She's bringing $800 cash. She'll be here in fifteen minutes.' Can you handle that?"

"My ma wants to buy—"

"You better say *mom* instead of *ma*. You're supposed to sound innocent."

"My mom wants to buy. She's bringing $800 cash. She'll be here in fifteen minutes."

"You talk good, kid. Now listen to what the scam's about in case you have to wing something. See Johnny keeps a couple a piss-cars—beaters as worthless as a pair of tits on a dead hog—parked in the back corner of the lot. Anyone with half a nose'll run the other way if they see these moose shits, so he keeps them pretty much out of sight. One we paint red, right over the rust. Worse than a Scheiber, takes me maybe an hour. We also spank a couple red floor mats down and hang a little cherry air freshener, maybe put on some red seat covers. Other than that we leave it sit."

"Paint over rust? Who'd buy that?"

"Let me tell you something, kid. Every car's got a buyer. And the condition of the car don't mean shit. It's the condition of the *buyer* that counts. The condition of the buyer and the scam. You match your scam to the condition of your buyer and you can sell anything with air in the tires."

"What kind of buyer—"

"A broad. A single one. A single broad steps on this lot and we got her. Johnny puts on his plaid sportcoat and smile and a second later he's out there with his arm around her asking how much she can afford to spend. Say she says five hundred. Johnny flashes five fingers with the arm that's around her so I can see it from the window here. That's how I got the $800 figure for your little spiel: took what she can afford and tacked on $300. If he flashes four fingers, you say $700. If he flashes seven—"

"I say a grand."

"You add good, kid. Only don't say *grand* when you do the spiel. Say a thousand dollars. Grand sounds like you're mob or something."

"A thousand dollars."

"But you don't say jack until Johnny leads her to that back corner. And see he don't push the red car. He walks her past it and starts hard-selling the other turd. 'It's a runner,' he tells her. 'At five hundred it's a peach of a value. May not look good but it runs out well'—all that stuff broads don't give a cunt fart about. He hasn't even started it and you can bet your little wrinkled sack-a-marbles she's eyeing the red one. 'How much for this one?' she'll say. 'Seven hundred,' he says. 'But there you're paying for reliability *and* looks.' Two hundred more for a nice red car, the broad thinks. Johnny opens the door, she smells the air freshener, you come running and—"

"My mom wants to buy. She's bringing $800 cash. She'll be here in fifteen minutes."

"Broad'll take one look at you and write a check for eight-fifty. She'll shove it in Johnny's face and beg him to sign it over. Johnny's all of a sudden looking like a nice-guy referee instead of the bullshitter he is. When he adds the fake tax and dealer preparation charges, she don't think twice about it. She ends up paying a grand-plus when she can only afford five hundred, so Johnny finances two-three hundred at a fine print 10% a month. See when a broad's competing with another broad, she loses her head. They're like sharks, these broads, with the red paint like blood."

The Barricade

Norb Hike spent weekdays on his worm farm. Saturdays were the day he lived for—the day he came alive as a used car man.

"Now Johnny," he told me and Gary during a Saturday morning break in the tool crib, "is the best used car man ever. Talk about looks? He's got the ducktail. Talk about clothes? A different paisley tie for every day of the week. Talk about mouth? More lines than a ream a looseleaves. He's got everything, and he's got more of everything than anyone. But you know what Johnny does that puts icing on his cake? He *reads* people. Like they're directions on a shampoo bottle. Buying or selling, the sonofabuck always knows exactly what the other guy's thinking. The other guy's desperate, Johnny'll read it. The other guy's lying, Johnny'll read it. The other day he was on the phone with this mob guy in Chicago and—"

"*Hike.*"

We looked up.

Liquid Johnny stood in the doorway that led to the showroom, frowning.

Gary stepped on the scale.

"You got a second?" Liquid Johnny said.

"Sure, Chief," Norb Hike said, and he walked into the contract signing room just off the showroom. Liquid Johnny followed, closed the door behind them.

Gary stepped off the scale shaking his head. "On the *nog*gin."

Half an hour later I was cruising south on Highway 41 in Norb Hike's good used '58 Rambler. The upholstery was wrapped twice with clear sandwich plastic. Norb Hike was driving.

"Damn clean car," I said. The speedometer read 104. "Rides smooth."

"As a shitter, hey?" Norb Hike said. "Cost me three hundred bucks." He leaned back, plastic crackling. He curled his lower lip over itself. "Used the old barricade scam to get it."

The speedometer read 11O.

"Barricade scam?"

"Gary never mentioned that one?"

"No."

"Johnny probably told him not to. Some things in this business are sacred."

The speedometer needle pressed on: 116.

"But you know what, kid?" he said. "You're gonna be a helluva used car man someday. Maybe even better than me. And that's why I'm gonna tell you about the barricade scam. All I ask is that when I'm down there being worm feed, you find some kid . . . and do the same for him that I done for you. And not just any kid . . ."

The '58 Rambler began losing speed.

"Mr. Hike?"

"Huh."

"You were saying?"

"*Oh.* Yeah. The barricade scam. First thing you do is hunt yourself down a good runner in the classifieds. You know: low miles, desperate situation."

"Like any good used car man does."

"Exactly. But here's how you *get* the runner before the rest of 'em—and cheap. You call the seller as soon as you've found the ad and tell him to hold onto the car because you're ready to pay cash. Then you drive to wherever the car is, check her over to make sure she's a runner, and low-offer the seller."

"Low-offer?"

"You know, floor-dollar the guy. Offer him an ounce of piss when he's asking a gallon of honey. Take this-here Rambler. Cherry car, obviously. Seller was desperate—wife just had triplets. I call and get down there and he's asking twelve hundred. I look him straight in the eye and counteroffer half-a-half-a that, three Ben Franklins staring him right in the face."

"And he took it?"

"Told me to go to hell on a bobsled. But he got an eyefull of them C-notes. See it's very important to let a guy eye the green."

"Like red with women?"

"Like red with—say *broads*, kid. You're growing up."

"Broads. So how'd you get him down from twelve hundred?"

"That's where your barricades come in. See, after you leave the seller, you barricade a few of the streets the guy gave you in his directions. Of course you use them city barricades, the kind with CONSTRUCTION or BRIDGE OUT signs on them, to make sure other buyers don't just move 'em aside and drive on. Plus you put little handwritten signs on them—like 'RAMBLER SOLD' if you're trying to buy this-here car?—just to make sure."

"You steal the barricades?"

"*Borrow* 'em, kid. A used car man never steals."

"Then what."

"Then let the other boys call the seller for the rest of the day. The seller gets all these calls but no one's stopping by, so he figures his price is too high. And if he's sitting in waiting for callers and visitors, chances are he'll never go out and see the barricades."

"When do you go back?"

"Late that night. You send your wife. You're gonna have to get yourself a wife someday, kid. You give the wife a buck more than you offered and have her tell some sob story about needing wheels."

"Works every time?"

"Not every. Sometimes they find the barricades. Sometimes they hold their price. But if they're in a must-sell situation, you got yourself a runner."

His lower lip curled over itself and stayed that way until we stopped at the property where my dead grandfather had bought his '33 Pontiac.

Then it moved:

"Liquid don't want you sleeping in the tool crib no more. So I'll let you live down here."

"You own this property?"

"It's my worm farm, kid."

We got out of the good used '58 Rambler. Wind swished the elm tree branches. We walked toward the farmhouse. The German shepherd came running.

"Down, bitch."

"Down, bitch."

Norb Hike opened the door. We walked into the kitchen. A guy sat on a folding chair beside a card table, hunched away from us, legs crossed, an arm on the table like five pounds of salami. A pack of Chesterfields and a cereal bowl sat beside his arm.

"This is Mike," Norb Hike said.

"Mike."

Mike lit a Chesterfield. His head was shaped like a light bulb: large forehead-and-ears funneling into a pimply chin.

Norb Hike looked at me. "He don't talk. Can't hear, either. Ran away from Chicago when he was a kid."

"Visiting?"

"Lives here. Works for Liquid Johnny in the woods."

"What's he do?"

"Gardening. Wholesale produce."

Mike's Chesterfield trembled. He smoked it, flicked ashes into his cereal bowl. There was another Chesterfield behind his ear, this one unlit and steady.

Norb Hike opened a cabinet and pulled out a burlap sack. "Don't mind him." He opened the sack, reached in, and grabbed a handful of puffed rice. "Eat as much of this as you want." He threw the handful in a sky blue garbage pail beneath the sink.

Then he opened the refrigerator. There appeared to be nothing inside it but silver—until I realized what I was seeing.

"That sure is a lot of foil."

"Individually wrapped olive loaf sandwiches," Norb Hike said.

"That sure is a lot of sandwiches."

"A hunnerd twenty count. That's two each a day for you and Mike for a month. One for lunch, the other for supper. In a month I'll bring a fresh stock. I make 'em myself."

I'd eaten olive loaf once. Once for a reason. "You shouldn't be so generous," I said.

"Oh, you're gonna earn this," Norb Hike said. He slammed the refrigerator door six times—and it held. "And you'll sleep anywhere you want in the joint. As long as you stay on the property, you'll be safe from The Authorities."

"How *do* I earn this?"

Norb Hike blinked a few times. "Run the worm farm."

He showed me the rest of the farmhouse, which—except for some spider webs—was empty, and then we went out back. The old cars were still there: rustier, with fewer doors, surrounded by taller weeds, waiting for Norb Hike to beat them with a tire iron and bulldoze them into a pond.

He walked through them to a clearing of clumped dirt

covered by pieces of wet cardboard. He held out an arm, palm up.

"Here she is."

"Who."

"My worm farm."

A shovel stood forked into the middle of the clearing. I nodded. "Why wet cardboard?"

"Keeps 'em close to the top. Moisture relaxes them. Panic Theory."

He stepped onto the cardboard, stood staring at the shovel. "Your job'll be watering the farm. And rotating the garbage."

"Garbage?" I stepped beside him.

He kicked aside a square of cardboard. I saw orange rinds, coffee grounds, wet newspaper, brown apple cores, nibbled pizza crust. "Worm food," he said, and he crossed his arms. "Every morning you clear the cardboard, rake the food around, replace the cardboard. Then water the works for an hour." He nodded at a shed across the clearing. "Rake and hose are in there."

"Piece a cake."

"You think so?"

I nodded.

"Then I got something else for you to do. For extra cash. And this is just between you and me."

"What's that."

He spread his feet, locked his knees, and held his hands apart—as if keeping a loaf of sliced bread between them. His hands bounced a few times and he spoke softly, almost whispered:

"See, I worry about straying. Worm straying. And I got this idea. But you gotta keep this secret."

"Shoot."

"There's twenty sheets a used sheet metal in that shack there. I wanna sink them all the way around the works, six foot deep." His hands kept bouncing. "Wire them with used extension cords, charge them with about 55O cold-cranking amps."

"An underground fence."

"Sharp idea, hey?"

"Sure will keep 'em from straying. How do I get the sheet metal in—soak the border and pound?"

"*God* no. Might cut a 'crawler in half that way. Wipe out the whole farm."

He stared at the shovel.

"No, kid, you're gonna have to dig a ditch all the way around. Carefully. And then *bury* the metal."

We stood for a minute.

"This is a delicate business, worm farming."

We stood for three minutes.

"Deal?"

"Sure."

Norb Hike winked and we shook hands. Then he got in his good used '58 Rambler and drove off.

I spent the rest of the day digging. I cut no nightcrawlers in half and buried one piece of sheet metal two and a half feet deep. This kept maybe four worms from straying. But for Norb Hike, it was worth it. It only cost him a bowl of puffed rice.

That evening I sat in the driver's seat of one of the rusty cars, imagining it had parts. I began *really* imagining—picturing a steering wheel in my hand and a broad beside me—when Mike appeared from the woods. The Chesterfield behind his ear was gone. Broccoli spears and green-topped carrots were under his armpit, sweet potatoes and parsley in his hands.

"Let's eat," the look on his face said.

Must be a garden beyond the woods, I thought. But then I saw a smudge behind his ear, where his Chesterfield had been. And it wasn't the chocolate color of Wisconsin garden dirt.

It was black—the death-nasty black of dirty motor oil.

The Woman

I was inside the ditch, digging. I'd been digging for months—and buried only eight pieces of sheet metal. Mike had been coming home with motor oil stains, which made me wonder, but not enough to investigate. I had my own problems: building the underground fence and how it would help me get back to Liquid Johnny's used car lot.

I kept digging. I was sort of my own boss but didn't like it. A car horn beeped and I stopped digging to look up.

Norb Hike's '58 Rambler rolled onto the farmhouse driveway, still mint.

"What a runner," I said to the ditch, wiping sweat off my neck. I thought about asking Norb Hike for a raise and settling for some commission used car work. Then the Rambler's door opened and a *woman* walked out: fat, with four shades of yellow hair.

My thoughts shuffled like pinochle cards suddenly cut: Gertie Hike.

I hadn't seen her since the day I ate my first third-of-a-steak at Norb Hike's bankrupt hardware store house. Now here she was, the same Gertie, just years fatter and with more shades of yellow hair.

I thought: My, she's grown into some kind of woman. I wanted to just stand there and look at the effect time and beer-drinking had had on her. But what if she recognized me and reported me to The Authorities? I ducked back into the ditch.

The car door slammed so hard I thought Gary had done it—until I remembered how Gertie had slammed doors as a youth. Then the farmhouse screen door slammed also. I peeked out from the ditch. Mike appeared from the woods, walked through the old cars with the German shepherd lacing itself between his legs. He held two dirty beets, had a Chesterfield behind his ear. He jammed the beets into his back pockets, pulled off his T-shirt, undid his pants button. The German shepherd nosed open the door. Mike turned, looked in my direction—and I ducked and the screen door slammed.

After a minute, I pulled myself out. I could spy through the farmhouse window on Gertie, Mike and the dirty beets, or hit the woods and investigate the motor oil thing.

I decided to hit the woods.

I ran down a path of wet leaves until I came to a fork. A sign was nailed to a tree: a black arrow pointing to the right.

Think like a used car man, I told myself, and I went left. The path zigzagged, narrowed, got darker. I was ready to turn back when I saw an old Quonset hut, a lot like the one behind Norb Hike's bankrupt corner hardware store house in Milwaukee, but completely scorched.

I thought: How many scorched Quonset huts can a guy buy in a lifetime?

I walked up to the door and tried it.

"Damn."

I walked behind the hut looking for windows. A new Lincoln Continental with Florida plates was parked there: white with red leather interior, one of those power-everything jobs. Its hood was open, engine gone.

A *new* car? I thought, and something sparkled behind some trees: fourteen new cars—Cadillacs and T-Birds and more Continentals—parked in a clearing.

Suddenly I heard barking. The German shepherd's a watchdog, I thought. And he's charging toward me through the woods. I sprinted to the fork, then blazed my own trail to the junkyard.

The used cars sat rusting, like old friends. Barks echoed through an open farmhouse window. I began sneaking through the cars to the underground fence ditch, watching the farmhouse in case the door opened. When it moved, I ducked behind an old Ford. I spied through a rust hole in the rear quarter panel, saw Gertie Hike walk to Norb Hike's good used '58 Rambler, each shade of her yellow hair looking combed.

The door opened again and spat Mike. His hair looked electrocuted. There was no Chesterfield behind his ear. There were two between his fingers, both lit and steady.

Gertie got in the good used '58 Rambler, didn't slam the door, then did. Mike stepped to the driver's side window, held the lit Chesterfields in front of her face. Her mouth took one.

Something bad's going on here, I thought, and the Rambler started, U-turned without signalling, and accelerated onto the driveway under the trees. Bad as used car exhaust, I thought, then noticed that the exhaust from the Rambler's tailpipe was clean.

Clean as a new Caddy, I thought.

3

The Rush

The underground fence was finished, plugged in, working. I was seventeen, no longer afraid of The Authorities, and tired as heck of puffed rice. I wanted to sell used cars.

But Norb Hike wouldn't stop talking:

"Know how I'm still losing worms?"

"No."

"Robins. Things peck the cardboard aside and suck out crawlers like the farm's a plate a leftover spaghetti. They're our biggest threat, robins."

"Mr. Hike—"

"We lick them robins and I could re*tire* off worms. And a dome is the answer. Like the ones they're gonna put over cities on the moon? But smaller. And fiberglass. Used, of course. I heard about an auction next month where—"

"I don't want to build a dome."

"What?"

"Nothing against worm farming. I just . . ."

"What."

"I wanna sell used cars."

Norb Hike looked at me as if we were the same age. "It's in your blood, hey?"

I didn't know what he meant. I nodded. "I wanna get back to the lot."

He coughed. "Can't do it."

"Why not."

"Can't say." He jammed a pinky in his ear, screwed it around in there, took it out, grabbed my shoulder. "Used cars can get pretty complicated, kid. Pretty dirty. You sure you don't wanna stick to worms? I'd make you partner someday."

His nostrils blinked like a frog's.

"Being partners would sure be something," I said. "But worms? I don't know. Worms aren't used cars. There's something about used cars . . ." My throat tightened. "Something inside me."

He squeezed my shoulder. "It's in your blood, kid."

An hour later he was driving me through downtown Milwaukee in his good used '58 Rambler. He put a dime on the dashboard. "See that phone booth?"

A phone booth stood on the corner.

"Yeah."

"That's where you'll go when I tell you to run."

I put the dime in my pocket. We rounded a corner, stopped in front of a building the color of Norb Hike's skin. He handed me a warm half dollar. "Use it. You'll know what for. I gotta park this." I got out and closed the door, and he sped away.

Nineteen men stood near the locked glass doors to the building as if they were a soupline: pacing, arms crossed, flicking dirt from beneath fingernails, smoking, wiping sweat off yellow foreheads, glancing at watches, the sun, the glass door, one another.

Used car men, I thought. I looked at a sign high on the side of the building:

THE MILWAUKEE JOURNAL

One of the glass doors opened. A stack of fresh classified ads was draped over a *Journal* employee's forearm. The used car men pressed toward him like housepets. Each had a quarter in his hand. I was right in the middle of them, holding Norb Hike's half dollar. The *Journal* employee took it. I grabbed my classifieds and a used car man with bloodshot eyes tried to tear them away from me. "Bastard," his eyes said.

I pushed through the crowd, stood on the curb, opened the paper. Norb Hike appeared around the corner, panting. His head was sweating but his pig-nose was flared and he was smiling. "Find anything?" he asked.

"Not yet."

He grabbed the paper, quartered it over his thigh, held the paper in front of his face, his stubby finger racing down the columns.

The other used car men did likewise, but Norb Hike was fifty cars ahead of all of them, easily. Then his finger stopped:

'56 T-BIRD. 8,OOO miles.
$25O or offer. 671-4693.

"Run," he said.

I ran around the corner to the phone booth, dialed the number, listened to fourteen rings and a number of phone-handling sounds.

"Yellow?" an old lady's voice crackled, like a Victrola. "Who's callink?"

"I'm calling about the car. Is it still for sale?"

"Car? Oh, ya. Car. Ya. It for sell. Ya."

"I'd like to come by and see it. Could you tell me your address?"

"Why sure. Two...fife. Six...tree. On da Lincoln Affanew."

"Twenty-five sixty-three Lincoln?"

"Ha? Two...fife..."

Norb Hike's good used '59 Rambler pulled up to the curb. His round head poked out the window. "Got the address?"

I nodded.

"Six...tree..."

Norb Hike spat on some curb garbage. "Tell her to hold."

". . . Lincoln Affanew."

"Could you hang on a minute, ma'am?"

"Why sure."

"Leave the phone off the hook," Norb Hike said.

I left the phone off the hook and got in the car.

Norb Hike pulled away. "Woman?"

"Yeah."

"Old?"

"Yeah."

"Senile?"

"Maybe."

He punched the accelerator. In minutes we were on Lincoln Avenue, standing on the front porch of a duplex, smiling at an aluminum door. Norb Hike knocked, kept knocking. No one answered. Blackened red rubberbands hung from the neck of the doorknob. I peeked through a lace curtain behind a window beside the porch. Cottage cheese cartons containing violet plants sat on the window sill. Behind them was a living room, dim like a cave but containing a fake-velvet couch, an end table and a black rotary phone. A white-haired woman bent like a cheese curl sat on the couch pressing the phone receiver against her ear.

"She's still holding," I said.

"It's *so* important to put them on hold," Norb Hike said.

"Keeps them awake." He kept knocking. "Freezes the competition, too."

I took over the knocking. Norb Hike scratched his crotch. The lace curtain moved and I heard sounds behind the door: clinking keys, stuck dead bolts, false starts on door-opening action. Norb Hike and I looked at each other. Finally the door opened. On the other side of the threshold was a three-legged aluminum cane supporting the oldest person I'd ever seen: blue-skinned, brown-spotted, shrunken like an apple doll.

Norb Hike blinked hard. "Afternoon, ma'am."

A green rubberband held a crumpled paper napkin to the old lady's wrist. "Who'ss diss?" she said. Her powder blue eyes were aimed well over our heads. For a second I thought there might be a tall used car man standing behind us, but no, the woman had cloudy patches over her eyeballs.

"We come to see your car," Norb Hike said.

"*Ha?*"

"WE COME TO SEE YOUR CAR."

"Oh, ya. Da car. Come in."

The lady put her three-legged cane in reverse and backed up about an inch per step to let us in. Two minutes later we were all standing in her living room. It looked less like a cave from the inside but smelled like good used car upholstery: violet plants.

There were violet plants everywhere: on all the windowsills, on the end table, on the bases of all four walls. Each violet plant sat in a cottage cheese carton.

That woman must have eaten a lot of cottage cheese.

She inch-stepped to the fake velvet couch, took almost a minute to position herself to sit, and less than a second to do the actual sitting. The cushion she sat on was smashed like a grilled cheese sandwich, its fake velvet almost slick bald. The other two cushions were fine.

She fingered a yellowed doily. "Can I fix it for you da . . . coffee?"

"NO, THANKS," Norb Hike shouted. "WE'D LIKE TO SEE THE CAR."

"Ha?"

"THE CAR. WE'D LIKE TO *SEE* THE *CAR.*"

"Ya, Ya. Da car." She rocked forward, half-stood, then fell back onto her cushion. I held out my hand to help her. She waved it off. "I do it myself." She rocked again and again, gained momentum, finally stood.

Norb Hike raised his eyebrows.

The old lady shifted her cane to drive and led us down a speckled linoleum hallway to her kitchen.

Her kitchen smelled like cold sauerkraut and contained a formica table, an ice box, and an electric stove. The table was scarred from knife blades. A pan of stone-cold sauerkraut sat on the ice box. The stove top was vacant but the right rear burner was orange hot.

The old lady stirred the cold sauerkraut with the wrong end of a fork. "I find it da keyss." She shuffled to a drawer beside the sink and began rummaging: pipe cleaners, a used tape dispenser, used birthday candles . . .

Norb Hike stepped to the stove, turned off the burner, gave me a wink. The old lady held a mousetrap in front of her face, dropped it in the drawer, and continued rummaging.

Half an hour later we were all in her garage. Her '56 T-Bird was mint as a new penny. Norb Hike started it with a flick of the wrist. The engine hummed. He winked at me, opened the hood, shook his head. "ENGINE'S SHOT."

"What you say?"

"YOUR ENGINE IS SHOT. I'LL GIVE YOU FIFTY DOLLARS FOR THE CAR."

"My car iss . . . no goot?"

"NOT GOOD AT ALL, MA'AM."

"Agh. It does me no goot anywayss. You no want it?"

"I'LL GIVE YOU FIFTY DOLLARS FOR IT. TAKE IT OFF YOUR HANDS."

"It does me no goot. You take it, for fifteen dollarss."

"YOU GOT A DEAL."

"You wannit da meal?"

"*DEAL.*"

"Ya, ya. Deal."

Minutes later we were in her bedroom, rifling through her dresser drawers for the title. Norb Hike found her last will and testament in a hatbox full of snap-on garters. He read the will, put it back under the garters. "Tempting."

I myself found a lot of yarn. Then I found the title, in a pillowcase behind some shawls and crocheting equipment.

Another inch-step parade and the lady was sitting at her formica kitchen table, signing.

As soon as she lifted her complimentary savings and loan

pen, Norb Hike took the title and headed for the front door.

"You pay it da money?" the old lady said.

Norb Hike stopped in his tracks. "No, ma'am." His face turned red. "I'm sorry."

His honesty surprised me. But then he took two one dollar bills from his wallet and placed them on the table, square in front of the old lady. "TEN AND TEN IS TWENTY. YOU GOT FIVE DOLLARS CHANGE?"

She held one of the bills less than an inch from her face, looked over her shoulder, in my direction. "Diss iss a ten?"

I didn't know what to say.

"YES, MA'AM," Norb Hike shouted from the other side of her.

The old lady looked at me and smiled: "I don't . . . see so goot no more." She began laughing, steadied herself by clutching her bosom.

Norb Hike laughed with her.

She stopped laughing, took the crumpled napkin from the rubber band around her wrist and coughed into it. "I gettit da chainch." She inch-stepped to a cabinet beneath the kitchen sink, got a purse, returned to her chair at the formica table. She must have been the type that had to be sitting to do business. She opened the purse: folded church bulletins, rumpled blue Kleenexes, a wad of oregano-green bills clipped together by a clothespin.

She pulled a twenty from the wad, held it over her eyes, looked over her shoulder in my direction. "Diss iss a fife?"

"NO," Norb Hike shouted. "THAT'S A ONE. FOUR MORE OF THOSE AND WE'LL BE SQUARE."

The old lady smiled in my direction, gave me the twenty, pulled out four more, handed them to me. "I don't see so goot no more," she said, and she laughed as if she'd just won the World Series.

"AT LEAST YOU STILL GOT YOUR SENSE OF HUMOR," Norb Hike said.

The old lady laughed harder, clutched her old reliable bosom, nodded. Norb Hike laughed with her. I almost chuckled myself.

She was still laughing when we left the duplex with the keys, the title, and ninety-eight dollars' profit.

"Coulda paid her with asswipe," Norb Hike said after she'd locked the front door. "But at some point, a guy's gotta be honest."

We started down the porch stairs. I stopped. "Think we should give her a twenty or so back?"

Norb Hike stopped. "Up to you, kid."

I turned, climbed the stairs, and knocked on the front door.

"You're a good man, kid," Norb Hike said. "You sure you wanna sell cars?"

I knocked again.

He looked through the lace curtain. "Ain't on the couch. Probably eating that sauerkraut."

"Think so?"

"Sure. You knocked enough, kid. You're clear. Besides, I got someplace else to take you. Gary'll get the car later."

We got in Norb Hike's good used '58 Rambler. He drove to a block of bungalows, a lot like the one my grandparents had lived in, but bigger. He parked in front of one of them. It looked like all the others.

"Where we going?"

"Casey and Josephine's."

"They selling or buying."

"You'll see."

We got out the car, walked into the bungalow without knocking, began walking on a plastic runner across a carpeted living room.

"What're we doing here?"

"Celebrating."

The plastic runner led us into another room, past a bowl of plastic red and green peppers on a used table, through an open doorway, down a curled flight of basement stairs.

The basement was crowded with 3Ps, cigar smoke, a pool table, two card tables, a pressboard bar, more cigar smoke. A 3P kid chasing a bouncing cue ball across the tile floor stopped suddenly, a used dog harness strapped around his chest and neck and leashed to a card table by fat gray clothesline, his mother sitting at the table drinking beer from a paper cup.

Norb Hike led me to the bar. A 3P couple stood behind it, erect and smiling. A man with a nose like a hawk's sat on a stool beside us.

Basement tavern, I thought. Gary had told me about them.

The man behind the bar wore a Pabst bowling shirt with an embroidered pocket:

CASEY

The woman beside him weighed enough to play for the Packers. She must have been Josephine. Norb Hike and I sat on some barstools. Josephine had on furry slippers the color of canaries. Casey pointed at an air conditioner beside a stuffed walleyed pike wearing a Milwaukee Braves baseball cap. "See our new cooler?"

Norb Hike looked at the air conditioner. It combed the few hairs on his head. "What more could you ask for?"

"A beer," I said, and everyone laughed.

It took awhile for them to stop laughing. Then Casey said, "What more could you ask for?"

"A *beer*!" Josephine said, and they laughed for another ten seconds.

I was making up for lost bar time quickly.

Casey poured a beer from a keg and set it in front of me. "A beer it is. First one's free."

"Price is right," I said, and everyone laughed as I sipped. The beer was bitter but easy to swallow. I drank it all down. Everyone got quiet.

The man with the hawk's nose was staring at me, a used paper cup and a half-empty pitcher in front of him. He made sitting on a barstool look comfortable. "*Woytek* can *drink*," he said, and everyone laughed louder than before.

I wanted to laugh with them, but couldn't. Laughing just didn't quite work for me.

"Two Pabsts," Norb Hike said, and Casey began pouring.

Five Pabsts later I felt comfortable on my stool. Norb Hike was playing darts. Two women came down the stairs, walked over to the dartboard, and began talking with Norb Hike. Cigar smoke hid their faces. Norb Hike opened his wallet, gave them cash. I thought: What's going on here?

The women began walking to the bar. The bigger one had many shades of yellow hair and was fat:

Gertie Hike.

She smiled at me, kept approaching. I pretended to care about a chain of bubbles rising in my beer. Now I might *really* make up for lost bar time, I thought.

"Couple tappers, Jo," a voice like a diesel mechanic's said: Gertie was standing next to me.

Josephine rose from her seat on a ten gallon potato chip tin, poured two picture-perfect Pabsts, displayed them on the bar smiling proudly. She was a beer-pouring artist, all 2OO pounds of her. She and Casey were set for life: they had a bar in their basement.

Gertie Hike grabbed one of the beers and slugged it down her drainpipe of a throat. The other beer sat there. "They get warm if you stare at 'em," she said to the other woman.

The other woman sipped the beer and winced. She had brown hair, all one shade.

Could she be? I wondered. *No*, I thought. She was too grown up, too beautiful to be the girl who'd once, in a bankrupt corner hardware store, sung "Somewhere Over the Rainbow" three times: Pam Hike.

"She don't drink much," Gertie Hike told Josephine.

Everyone got quiet.

Hawk Nose leaned forward, looked at the beautiful woman, wrinkled his purple forehead: "She a *nun* or something?"

Everyone laughed so loud my ears hurt.

"Easy, Zig," Gertie Hike said. "She's my kid sister. She's protecting her voice. She's gonna be a professional singer."

It's her, I thought. It's 100% Pam Hike.

Everyone looked at Hawk Nose.

"Or a professional talker," he said. "Like her old man."

Everyone laughed out of control, belching and farting.

Hawk Nose looked at me. "You ever laugh, *woytek?*"

I faked a laugh. Pam Hike watched me and smiled. I glanced away, pretending not to notice that her eyes were brown and soft, not at all like her sister's gray eyes, which looked like transplants from a dead northern pike.

I sipped some Pabst. Hawk Nose was telling a joke about three Italians. Billiard balls clicked. I watched cigar smoke surround Pam Hike's head like a halo. She was still looking at me and smiling, but like a private investigator—a private investigator with hair shiny and smooth as a fresh coat of brown high-gloss.

Maybe Gertie Hike could have had the same hair color without all those coats of peroxide, or the same girlish figure without all those cases of beer.

But I wasn't interested in The Hike Family Tragedy.

I was interested in Pam Hike.

". . . looks like cheese to me!" Hawk Nose said, and everyone laughed, except Pam Hike. She was looking at me, smiling.

Staring back at her, I sipped some Pabst, then swished it around my mouth as if it were mouthwash.

Her square teeth smiled. Her brown eyes laughed softly.

Laugh along, I thought. I swallowed my mouthful and faked a small giggle.

It was not a hard giggle to fake.

Cardboard Light Switches

Norb Hike began unlocking the four used deadbolts on the front door to his bankrupt hardware store house. There were about thirty keys on his door prize Miller High Life key chain. "Fixed the place up since the last time you seen it," he said. "Got seventeen rooms now."

I looked at the boarded-over storefront windows. Seventeen rooms seemed impossible. But then again it wasn't just anyone's bankrupt corner hardware store house. It was Norb Hike's.

He and I stood there alone. Pam Hike had followed Gertie out of Casey and Josephine's just before closing, probably for cheeseburgers. Norb Hike thighed open the door. We stepped into a closet-sized section of bankrupt hardware store. Its walls were sheets of cardboard staple-gunned to one another and hung from the stained ceiling by used yardsticks. A high-watt bulb above some other room cast just enough light for me to see Norb Hike grin and extend his arm.

"Sitting room."

"Nice."

The largest button I've ever seen was glued to one of the cardboard walls. I noticed razor cuts in the cardboard. Norb Hike grabbed the button, opened the homemade door.

"Button doorknob," I said, and I followed Norb Hike into the next section of old hardware store.

"Three for a nickel at the Seven Mile Fair," he said. His lower lip curled over itself. I still couldn't see the high-watt bulb.

The walls of this room were a lavender semi-gloss that almost hid the black shipping directions you'd expect on one side or another of cardboard.

Norb Hike made a fist in his pocket, jingled his spare change.

"Dining room?" I asked.

His shiny head nodded. He uncurled his lower lip. "Wife picked the color." He grabbed another large button, led me through another homemade door. A refrigerator stood in the next cardboard room.

"Kitchen," he said. He opened the refrigerator, grabbed a handful of grapes from a raw wood crate that covered the whole top shelf of the refrigerator, and crammed them into his mouth. "Loose grapes," he said, chewing. "A buck for the twenty pounds. I'd give these suckers another two days, if they're lucky. Have some."

I'd never seen twenty pounds of loose grapes before. Some were red, some were green, most were brown with gray fuzz where their stems had been. I grabbed and ate: jelly-sweet with rubbery skins.

Right then I decided to get things going with Pam Hike, and quickly. Norb Hike and I stood chewing. The smells of beer breath, smokey clothes and grape meat buried the cardboard scent of his bankrupt hardware store kitchen. I was excited about my future.

Norb Hike swallowed, then grabbed more grapes. Salad bowls of water on the second shelf contained nightcrawlers. He crammed his second handful of grapes in his mouth, nodded at the crate. "More?"

"No thanks."

He grabbed handfuls three and four as he chewed. "For the wife," he said, winking. "You wanna get that door?"

I grabbed the giant button on the next cardboard door. We stepped into a long cardboard hallway of about nine hanging bedsheet doors. It looked like a sleeper car of a train, but more likely was once a nut and bolt aisle of a hardware store.

Norb Hike yanked aside the first bedsheet to the left, revealing a toilet and sink on maybe ten square feet of floorspace. We were getting closer to the high-watt bulb. "Pisser," he said. He elbowed my ribs. "Beer's gotta go somewhere."

He led me to the next bedsheet down, yanked it open. The room was brightly lit and barely fit a twin mattress.

He stared at the mattress and nodded six times. "Guest room."

The mattress was striped except for some stains shaped like oysters. "Looks comfortable," I said. The high-watt bulb could have been one room over. I pointed at the stained ceiling. "Any way to turn that off?"

"*Oh* no," Norb Hike said. "That stays on. Flipping switches wastes juice, you know." He put his two handfuls of grapes on the wooden hall floor, stepped on the mattress and grabbed a piece of cardboard from against the cardboard wall. "If you want it dark in here . . ." He raised the piece of cardboard over his head. "You . . . put this . . . up here . . . like . . ." He slid the cardboard onto the tops of the walls. "Like *that.*"

The room was black as radiator hoses.

"If you wanna little night light, just slide her over a hair." Yellow light striped his baldness and some of the mattress.

"You think that up on your own?"

Norb Hike stepped from the mattress to the hall, began picking up grapes. "Sure. Meter man says we got the lowest reading on the block. Use less than the average blind person." He picked up his last grape and pointed down the hall. "The wife and I'll be behind the last sheet on the right." His eyes twinkled. "Master bedroom." He threw a grape against the back of his throat. "Think you'll need anything?"

"No."

He began down the converted hardware store aisle. "Have a good night, kid." He kept walking with his back to me. "You deserve it."

When he disappeared behind that last bedsheet I was alone, full of Pabst beer and loose grapes, hungry for Pam Hike and a future selling used cars.

I also had to use the bathroom.

While I used the bathroom I heard a pair of voices moving along the cardboard hallway. I first thought it was Norb and Joan Hike getting more grapes, but the deep voice was too low and the high voice could have been a professional singer's: it was The Hike Family Tragedy, Gertie, and her ripely beautiful sister, Pam.

The voices moved, faded, dissolved. I finished using the bathroom, walked to the guest room, and lay on the mattress, taped by the stripe of yellow light.

The converted hardware store grew silent as rubber washers. Then cooing swept the hall like a breeze: Pam Hike humming "Edelweiss."

I got up and stepped into the hall. "Edelweiss" was coming from behind one of the last bedsheets on the left. I took a soft step toward it. The floor creaked. "Edelweiss" stopped.

Scared her, I thought. Or maybe she knows I'm here and

this is more of the game we played in Casey and Josephine's.

I tiptoed to the last bedsheet on the left, pulled it aside. Directly beneath the high-watt bulb was Gertie Hike's ass. The rest of her was lumped asleep beneath a blanket, but there was her ass: large, cold, and alone, like a spare tire in a snowstorm.

I yanked closed the bedsheet.

"Edelweiss" began again, behind the next bedsheet over.

I stepped in front of it, pulled it open. Pam Hike sat cross-legged on her mattress wearing a used T-shirt and boxer shorts, probably Norb Hike's. She looked fresh and thin, like a cheese sandwich. She stopped humming "Edelweiss."

"Need something?" she said, smiling nervously.

I smiled nervously also. "Maybe."

Our nervous smiles blended into a very pleasant feeling, at least for me.

She stood. My steel-tipped shoes looked her clear-painted toenails square in the eye.

"You're Sophie's grandson, aren't you."

I hadn't expected that one. "Maybe," I said nervously, without smiling.

"You, Sophie and Stanley came over here to eat steaks."

"When."

"Long time ago. When Stanley was alive."

"I don't remember."

"Yes, you do. I sang for everyone that night. 'Somewhere Over the Rainbow.' Three times."

I pretended to clear my throat. I didn't want Pam Hike to know me from my past as a poor grandchild, but from my future as a rich used car salesman. "You sure you got the right guy?"

"Positive. We had steaks. I'd just gotten a haircut. You sat there like you had better things to do. Remember?"

"Maybe."

"I ate a third of your steak. It was your first one ever. Mine, too."

"Steaks. Hmmm . . ."

Pam Hike recharged her nervous smile. "You don't talk much, do you."

"Depends."

"You're scared of girls, aren't you."

"No."

She stood on her striped mattress, then stepped toward me. "Then kiss me."

The only women I'd ever kissed before were old fat ones: friends of my grandmother. I grabbed Pam Hike's tiny waist and kissed her lips best I could. Her eyes fluttered, as they had when she'd sung all those years ago:

Some. WHERE. Over. The rain-BOW . . .

I finished the kiss. Pam Hike opened her eyes and wiped her mouth with the back of her hand. "You were nervous."

"Not at all."

"You're scared of girls."

I thought of Kasha the Healer. "Impossible."

"You *are*. I can tell. You're scared of girls on account of what your mom did to your dad."

"What?"

"You *know*."

"No I don't."

"You do *too*."

I liked the way Pam Hike's lips said "too," so I kissed them. Again, her eyes fluttered. "Don't kid me like that," I said. "My mother died of scarlet fever right after I was born and left me with my father. My father was a used car salesman. He got killed in a car wreck, test-driving a trade-in."

"Who told you that?"

"A friend."

"That's not what your grandmother told my mother."

"Don't kid me about this."

"I'm not. That's not at all what she told my mother."

"What she tell your mother?"

"I'm not supposed to say."

"Says who."

"Gertie."

"What's she have to do with it?"

"She's the one who told me everything."

"You said my grandmother told your *mom* everything."

"She did, ten years ago. Five years later my mom told Gertie. Last year Gertie told me."

"So it's a rumor."

"It's a *true* rumor."

"But my friend told *me* my mother died of scarlet fever."

"What's this friend's name?"

"Malcolm."

"The Indian Lady's?"

"Yeah."

"Who you gonna believe: what your grandmother told a neighbor, or an ex-con?"

Pam Hike had a point there. She was a good talker, like her father. She was the kind of girl a guy could settle down and sell used cars with.

I kissed her like a plunger.

Her eyes fluttered.

The kissing part was working out well.

"I won't believe anything 'til I hear it," I said.

"But I'm not supposed to tell."

I kissed her again, moved my tongue around in there. Her mouth watered into mine and I pulled away.

"I'd hate to go back on my word," she said.

I looked her in the eye. It was brown, soft and part of a matching set.

"Gertie would kill me if she knew I told."

I ran my fingers through her brown fresh-coat-of-high-gloss hair.

"I'd hate to disappoint her," she said.

"Who'd you rather disappoint: your beer-drinking sister, or me?"

"I'll have to think that one over." She turned, grabbed a piece of cardboard from between her mattress and wall, lifted the cardboard over her head. Her girlish leg and arm muscles stretched as she stood on her toes to lid the room. I thought of panthers, and when the room went black I thought of other animals also. Norb Hike was quite an inventor.

"The dark make it easier to think things over?" I asked.

"Yeah. That and other things."

Our fingertips groped, tickled each other's faces. We bumped foreheads softly, barely touched lips, and kissed, breathing through our noses and teeth. Her breath tasted nothing like a panther's, Pabst beer, or cheeseburgers. It tasted like Pam Hike.

"I see what you mean," I said. "Now tell me what you heard about my parents." I grabbed her warm hand, pulled down gently. We sat on the mattress cross-legged and faced each other's voices.

"Do I have to?" her voice said. Her hand squeezed mine. I smelled her perspiration. It was fresh and sweet and I remembered we were sitting inside what was more or less a cardboard box.

My hand squeezed hers. "Must be important if I'm asking now."

"Sure *must* be."

A pause filled itself with hand-squeezing and the fresh smell of Pam Hike.

Finally she said: "Your father . . ."

"Go on."

"Had blue eyes. Like marbles."

"That have anything to do with what my mom did?"

"No. But Gertie did tell me that."

"Get to the tough stuff.

Pam Hike squeezed my hand. "Your mother . . ."

"Just say it."

She squeezed my hand harder. "Liquid Johnny—"

"What's *he* got to do with it?"

"He used to sell used cars with your father."

"I know."

"Your father did all the brain work. Liquid Johnny got all the glory."

"So?"

Pam Hike squeezed my hand, kept squeezing. "Your father caught your mother in the back seat of a used Cadillac. With Liquid Johnny."

I had a very hard time figuring out what to say next. Talk like a used car salesman, I thought. "What year Cadillac?" I asked.

"Forty-eight."

"This happen before I was born?"

"Right after. So then your father tried to squeeze Liquid Johnny out of the business. Liquid turned around and got your father in trouble. Made it look like he'd stolen mob money. Your father had to leave town. In a hurry."

"I don't believe this."

"I'm not asking you to."

"What about my mother?"

"*She* was killed test-driving a car. For Liquid. After your father left."

"That's terrible. But I guess she deserved it."

"It's all terrible. That's why your grandparents never told you. They never told anyone, your mother being their daughter and all. Until your grandmother told my mother."

"I guess she had to tell someone."

Pam Hike squeezed my hand. I leaned forward, kissed her,

let my fingers touch the bangs of her brown-coat-of-paint hair. We lost our cross-legged balance onto the mattress, kissing, touching and rolling. Our legs tangled and knotted themselves, and then our bodies shifted like an automatic transmission into twisting and slithering.

Pam Hike pulled away. "You want to leave Milwaukee and find your father, don't you."

I listened to her breathe.

"Yeah," I said, and I sparked a new kiss.

Then I cut the kiss.

"And sell used cars," I said.

Alley Bowling

We'd circled the Pulaski Park lagoon, watching turtle heads disappear from the chrome surface.

"I need a good used car," I said. "Or I'll never find him."

We circled the lagoon again, saw nothing but floating sticks.

"Enough turtles," Pam Hike said. "Let's take a lawn ornament walk."

"Gettin' dark," I said.

She slid her arm under mine, grabbed my biceps. "So?"

We began walking, ended up in a 3P neighborhood of long brick houses with longer shadows.

"I bet management lives around here," I said.

We walked two blocks.

"Lawn ornament," Pam Hike said, pointing.

A plastic rabbit sat near someone's rosebushes.

"Cute," I said. We kept walking. Shadows began connecting houses.

"There's another," Pam Hike said.

A cement Virgin Mary stood under a half-buried used bathtub, praying.

"Beautiful."

We walked a block.

"LOOK AT THE DUCKIES!"

A line of little ducks were following a big duck to a wooden wishing well. The ducks weren't moving. We were.

"How 'bout that wishing well?" Pam Hike said.

"Carpenter must live there."

"How 'bout ahead on the right?"

A jockey stood near someone's front porch, smiling and waving. His skin was black as beetles, and ceramic.

"African jockey," Pam Hike said. We kept walking.

Then I saw it: a red metallic ball on a concrete stand designed like a courthouse pillar. I pointed, stopped walking. "What's that?"

Pam Hike opened her mouth. We walked toward the red metallic thing. "Looks like a . . ." We kept walking. "A *ball*."

We reached the yard, stopped, faced the red metallic ball like altar boys. The sun was about down.

"Size of a bowling ball," I said.

"Bet it's expensive," Pam Hike said.

I grabbed her hand and pulled. We walked half a block. She stopped. "Go get it."

"What."

"That ball."

"Me?"

"You're the *guy*."

"But I don't want a metallic ball lawn ornament. I don't have a lawn. I can't even afford a good used car."

Pam Hike looked around, ran back to the yard, grabbed the ball off the stand and ran back hugging it and smiling. "This is fun." Distant headlights lit up her face. "Oh Jesus." She stuffed the ball under her blouse and looked pregnant.

The car passed.

"I don't like this," I said.

She took the ball out from under her blouse, began walking. "Let's get one for you."

We walked a few blocks.

She pointed with her chin. "There's a blue one."

"You must have good eyes."

"Two carrots a day."

We walked ahead. The lawn ornament was blue all right. "Anyone around?" I asked.

"No."

I ran onto the lawn, grabbed the blue mirrored ball, ran back to Pam Hike. "These suckers are heavy." We walked two blocks. "What do *I* do if a car comes?"

"Drop it and run."

We walked six blocks to my grandmother's neighborhood. The streetlights came on. Pam Hike led me to the bottom of a familiar hill: Anna's alley. She set down her lawn ornament, opened an ash can, stuck her arms and head inside, came out with a large red can with a mustard-yellow man on it: Hills Brothers.

"Alley bowling," she said, setting the can on a sewer grate. She lifted her lawn ornament and began walking up the alley.

I tucked my lawn ornament under my arm and ran ahead

144

to Anna's garage. Two of her seven garage door windows had cracks like spider webs. I shaped my hands into a pair of binoculars, used them to spy through an uncracked one.

Larry's good used '49 Tudor sat there, looking exactly like it had when Norb Hike convinced my grandfather not to buy it. Pam Hike put her nose against the window beside me.

"What a runner," I said.

"My dad owns that car."

He's done it again, I thought. "Then why's it still here?"

"Free storage."

We quit spying. The tip of Pam Hike's nose was smudged with garage window dust.

"Know who gets the title when I marry?"

I scratched my head.

She raised her eyebrows.

I smiled.

She ran up the alley.

I lifted my lawn ornament over my head, chased her, caught up to her at the top of the alley, set my lawn ornament on a driveway, put my arms around her. Her lawn ornament was between us. "No smooching till we finish playing," she said. Her lawn ornament pushed me off. "You go first."

I picked up my lawn ornament, stepped to the middle of the alley, and bowled. Halfway down the alley the ball hooked to the left into a telephone pole. Blue mirrored glass flew everywhere.

"God," Pam Hike said. "You're *bad.*"

She stepped to the right side of the alley, crouched down, held her lawn ornament in front of her dusty nose. She took a few steps, bowled. Her lawn ornament started slowly, angled toward the middle of the alley, reflected red streetlight as it picked up speed, knocked over the can and stopped in a tomato patch.

She stuck out her chest, rubbed her hands together as if they were flints. "Nailed that sonofagun, didn't I."

I put my arms around her. "How'd you like to help a guy find his long-lost father?"

She licked her lips, closed her eyes. We kissed. She kept her fluttering eyes closed, smiled and—finally—nodded.

Key Advice

The reception would have been beneath Coz Brothers Bowl, but the Coz brothers were waxing lanes that afternoon.

The reception was in St. Josaphat's Bingo Hall, right after a cub scout meeting.

We entered the hall. A pack of cub scouts got an eyeful of my bride, Pam. She was beautiful and the cub scouts were becoming heterosexual citizens of our nation.

My grandmother was in the hall. So were Anna, Helen Pickadilly, the Indian Lady, Fommy, Father Pat, Gary, Liquid Johnny, Mike, Joan Hike, Gertie Hike, Norb Hike, and about thirty old neighbor people who waddled and sat around like molting ducks near a shade tree.

A half-barrel of beer was on tap. Gertie Hike was drunk and three pounds heavier in an hour. Mike sat at a card table smoking Chesterfields. Gertie never spoke to him, but he didn't seem to mind.

My grandmother and Helen Pickadilly sat near the dart board eating potato salad and purple jello like the best of friends.

This-Here-Malcolm never showed. Maybe he was in Waupun State Prison.

Soon the half-barrel began spitting foam. Norb Hike put his arm around me, walked me away from the folding chairs and old duck people, pulled a pair of keys from his pocket. "You know that friend of your grandma's, Anna?"

I scanned the folding chairs until I saw the combination of silver bifocals, age spots and stained paper plate that was Anna. "Yeah."

Norb Hike watched her while he talked out of the side of his mouth: "You remember that good used '49 Ford Tudor she had in her garage—the one we looked at with your grandfather?"

"Yeah."

He slapped two keys onto my palm. "Title's in your name, kid. Take good care of my little girl."

Tears crowded my eyes. I had to look at Anna to control them. "That car's a *runner*. It's worth big dough."

Norb Hike kept his eyes on Anna also. "That don't mean it cost much."

I looked at him like any misty-eyed used car man would: quickly. "Thanks, Dad."

"Call me Norb, kid. You still got a dad to find. And I hope you find him. He was quite a dealer. Just between you and me, I'd rather work with him than with Liquid."

"Is that right?"

"Sure. And kid? Before I forget. A few words about marriage."

"I'm all ears."

"Know what happens the first time you hear the wife use the toilet?"

"What's that."

"The honeymoon's over."

Two Saucers

It was a honeymoon of driving.

I drove Pam in my good used '49 Tudor through Beloit, a town straddling the Wisconsin-Illinois border.

As we crossed the border, there was something different about the faces on the drivers coming at us.

Pam was the first to mention this:

"You see that look on his face?"

"Butter smuggling."

"I should have figured."

That was all we said driving through Beloit.

I kept driving until we needed gas, in the Quad Cities.

Actually you can't stop in all the Quad Cities. On a map the Quad Cities are corners of a square, like a negative of a photograph of a domino laid across the Illinois-Iowa border. You can stop on only one dot at a time: just one Quad City.

The Quad City we stopped in was Moline. The other Quad cities are Rock Island, Bettendorf and the most famous Quad City, Davenport.

I couldn't find a phone booth in Moline, so I pulled up to the only place open: The Moline Titty Bar.

I got out of my good used '49 Tudor. Pam was still wearing her wedding dress. "Where you going?"

"Check the phone book."

"Keep your eyes off those titties."

I walked inside The Moline Titty Bar and didn't look at titties, just checked a phone book for my father's name, Wirzhbinski.

It wasn't listed.

"Each Quad City has its own phone book," a dancer holding coffee saucers over her titties told me.

"Oh."

"Looking up someone is no one-two-three task."

"That's funny, ma'am."

"How'd you like to look up me?"

"Thanks, but no."

"Ten bucks."

"Sorry."

"Five."

"Can't."

"Three for a titty squeeze?"

"Not today."

"How 'bout a quick peek. A buck a saucer."

"I got a wife in the car."

"*Now* you tell me."

I left the titty bar, got in my good used '49 Tudor. A roll of pink toilet paper and a J.C. Penney shoebox full of used breadbag ties sat on Pam's lap. A piece of pink toilet paper was wrapped around her finger. "Get what you wanted?"

I pinched my ignition key. "Didn't want anything."

She slid the toilet paper off her finger, wrapped a used green bread bag tie around the opening, threw the whole thing over her shoulder. "I mean the phone number."

"Oh. No." I let go of the ignition key. "What're you *doing*?"

"My crafts." She tore off a square of toilet paper, did the same thing with it that she'd done with the other, held it out at me. "What's this look like?"

"Piece a toilet paper."

"You men. Don't it look like a rosebud?"

"Sort of."

"Cute, inna?" She put it under my nose. "Smell."

I sniffed, didn't smell anything, and nodded. She threw the thing over her shoulder. Now there were two pieces of toilet paper on my back seat. I cleared my throat. "What you gonna do with those?"

"Sell 'em at St. Josaphat's bazaar. Penny apiece."

"What's it cost to make one?"

She lifted the toilet paper roll with one hand, the shoebox of used bread bag ties with the other. "Twenty-one cents for the thousand sheets, tax included. The ties I saved—free."

"But Josaphat's gets the profit."

"Josaphat's gets a third, I get a third."

"And the third third?"

"Father Pat."

"Is that why he kissed you like that at the reception?"

Pam tore off a square of toilet paper.

I started my good used '49 Tudor, drove off, then checked phone books in Rock Island, Bettendorf, and Davenport.

There were no Wirzhbinskis in the Quad Cities.

And Davenport was nothing special: not even a titty bar.

"I'm glad we didn't find him here," I said as we left Davenport.

Pam reached for a used bread bag tie. "Why's that."

"A used car man likes to think his long-lost father lives someplace exotic."

She threw a toilet paper rosebud over her shoulder. "Like where."

"I don't know. Nevada?"

Nevada

I was still driving. Pam had her craft raw materials on her lap and was really turning out the toilet paper rosebuds.

"You're on a roll," I said.

She tore off a pink square. "Roll's on *me*."

I saw a sign:

ENTERING NEVADA

We entered Nevada. It wasn't the exotic Nevada. It was Nevada, Missouri: a gas station with ninety-five octane level gas at twenty-eight cents a gallon.

My good used '49 Tudor guzzled that gas like a potted cactus.

Of course there wasn't a single cactus in Nevada, Missouri, potted or otherwise. There was rain, mud the color of peanut butter, and a payphone with a dog-earred, sun-yellowed white pages.

I had to stand in the rain and mud to get a look at the white pages.

"For gosh sakes," I said: someone had torn out the W's.

I had to call the Nevada, Missouri operator for the word on the W's:

"Nevada operator."

"Do you have any Wirzhbinskis listed?"

"Washburns?"

"Wirzhbinskis."

"Oh, *that* way. Did you check a phone book?"

"Yes. There's no W's in it."

"No W's? Check again. Nevada has columns of W's."

"Not here. Looks like someone tore them out."

"That again?"

"What do you mean, that again."

"Never mind. I'm just talking. Can you spell the name?"

"Yes."

"Out loud?"

I spelled Wirzhbinski.

"I'm sorry. No Wrishirekow—none of those listed."

I began wondering about this torn-out W's business.

I got back in my good used '49 Tudor. Pam was asleep, a toilet paper rosebud in her lap, her face flush against her wedding veil like a blind angel in a butterfly net.

The Bites

We were a mile outside of Bandera, Texas, and I'd driven twenty-nine and a half hours. Pam lifted the edge of her wedding veil. "This thing is making me warm."

I rolled down my window. Everything went pink.

"MY PROFITS! ROLL UP THE WINDOW!"

I rolled up the window. Toilet paper rosebuds covered the front seat, the floor, the dashboard, and Pam's veil.

"I want out of this dress."

Sounds good, I thought, and I drove my good used '49 Tudor into Bandera. I parked next to a plank-wood sidewalk, and the bowed legs of a cowboy grew larger in my rear-view mirror. I turned to Pam, pretended I was stirring the air. She rolled down her window. The cowboy walked past it.

"Say, buddy," I said.

Red tobacco juice arched from his mouth like a roller-coaster. Pam threw a handful of toilet paper rosebuds on the backseat.

"Say, BUDDY."

The cowboy stopped, backed up, ducked, looked through the passenger window at me, the backseat, and then Pam. There was a black cowboy hat on his head.

"What's the temperature?" I said.

"Hunnerd four, hunnerd five."

"Where's the Flying S Ranch Resort?"

The cowboy was still looking at Pam. He spit over his shoulder, then glanced at me. "You got business at the Flying S?"

It seemed like my turn to look at Pam, so I gave her a good one. Then I looked at the cowboy's shoulder, the one he'd spat over. It was clean as a fresh spark plug. "Yeah."

Wind rolled a tumbleweed across the road. The cowboy

grabbed his hat. "Hang a left at the sign, go 'bout three an a half mile to the gravel road, take *it* left, turn the first right, then the second left, then take the dirt about three quarter of a mile, and bear right at the fork. There'll be a sign. You can't miss it."

Pam rolled up her window. I hung a left at the sign, went about three and a half miles to the gravel road, took *it* left, turned onto the first right, then the second left, took the dirt road about three quarters of a mile, and bore a right at the fork.

There was a sign. I missed it.

Then I backed up, found the sign, and finally stopped in front of an office. I cut the engine, got out, walked into the office, coughing from road dust. A man in a western shirt and bluejeans stood looking out a dusty window at my good used '49 Tudor. A balloon-shaped belly hung over his snakeskin belt but his ass was the size of a throw pillow. His copper hair was sweaty and flat against his head. A gray cowboy hat sat on the registration counter like a lap dog.

I coughed one last good one. "I'd like a honeymoon cabin."

The man kept looking out the window. "Sir?"

"A *hon*eymoon cabin."

"None vacant."

"Then a regular cabin."

The man kept looking out the window. "None vacant."

"Listen, friend. I drove all the way from Wisconsin."

"I see that."

"That doesn't mean anything to you?"

"Means you ain't from Texas."

I glanced out the window myself, saw Pam tear off a piece of pink toilet paper in my good used '49 Tudor. "I'll level with you, pal. I just got married. Yesterday afternoon. I've been driving ever since."

"I can read license plates."

"That doesn't mean anything to you?"

The man finally looked at me. "Means you can rent my last campsite for five dollars."

"Five dollars? I saw motel rooms for *three*."

"You see them on the Flying S Ranch Resort?"

"No. But—"

"Campsite here'll set you back five. If that don't suit you, drive to one of them motels and do what you have to do for three."

"You moonlight selling new cars?"

"Sir?"

"Never mind. Here's your fivespot. You got a phone book?"

"Yella?"

"White."

"You huntin' down someone in particaler?"

"Wirzhbinski."

"Again?"

"Wirzh *bin*ski."

"That a Swedish name?"

"Polish."

"I'll tell you right off there's no Polish in Bandera. Up in Pawelickville there's a few Polish, but not in these parts."

"Could I check the book anyway?"

"Suit yourself. You won't find no Polish, though. I'll tell you what you need to do to find this fella. You need to go to Pawelickville. If this fella's Polish and in Texas, he's in Pawelickville. I'll guarantee it."

There were no missing pages in the Bandera, Texas phone book.

There weren't any Wirzhbinskis, either.

"You need to go to Pawelickville, is all."

I gave the man his white pages and looked out the window. Pam was tying a rosebud.

"Where's my campsite?" I said.

"You'll need for me to lead you. Let me get m' truck keys."

The balloon-bellied cowboy drove a '51 Chevy Pickup with polished steer horns on the hood and a gunrack on the back window. A shotgun lay in the gunrack like a toothpick in a dispenser, and we followed it.

The five-dollar campsite was the last of the campsite row, between an outhouse and a dump. The outhouse smelled like ammonia. The dump was full of bald tires and old vinyl couches with oatmeal colored stuffing seeping out of them like cauli-flower hernias.

Pam got out of my good used '49 Tudor, lifted her wedding dress over her ankles, walked to the outhouse, shut herself inside.

The balloon-bellied cowboy did a U-turn over our campsite, then pulled up alongside me. He sat high inside his pickup, idling. "You'll hear hoofs come sundown."

"Horses?"

"Deer. A mess a little does. If you hear gunshots, lay low and relax. I aim for their eyes. You'll be a good four foot under my line of fire."

The balloon-bellied cowboy drove away. I gathered some twigs from beneath the huisache trees around the dump. The sun set. I returned to the campsite. Lying spread on the middle of the campsite was a blanket from my good used '49 Tudor, Pam sitting on it like a centerpiece in stretchpants and an embroidered blouse.

I made a campfire. Pam got four half-price hotdogs from the styrofoam cooler she'd packed in Milwaukee. The hotdogs were red, spongy and wet from ten pounds of melted ice.

We fried the hotdogs on a flat rock in the middle of the campfire. They became dry, but black and crispy.

We ate a few bites of burnt hotdog.

Then we decided to clean up:

"Should we save the leftovers?"

"If we want them for breakfast."

I threw the leftovers in the nearby huisache trees and sat on the blanket, next to Pam. She began rubbing her shoulder against mine. My shoulder rubbed back.

Her shoulder stiffened. "I have to use the john."

"Good thing we have the outhouse."

"No outhouse for me in the dark. Snakes!"

"Good thing we have the huisache trees."

Pam used roughly the same huisache trees I'd thrown the burnt hotdogs in. The huisache trees were thick, but not so thick that I couldn't hear Pam using them. I thought: The honeymoon's *over?*

Pam returned to the blanket, and I decided to use the huisache trees myself.

I used roughly the same huisache trees Pam did. I was smack in the middle of using them when I heard a crunching sound at my feet. I looked down. An armadillo was chewing a burnt hotdog, looking at me like a shy child caught smoking a cigar.

Whistling "Deep in the Heart of Texas," I finished using the huisache trees. Then I took off my clothes, hung them on a branch, and returned to Pam. Our shoulders began rubbing again. I stopped whistling "Deep in the Heart of Texas." Soon her stretchpants were a wrinkled ball at her feet, and I was kneeling between her legs kissing her unused parts. Now she *really* tasted like herself. I kissed and watched her eyes flutter until she lifted the back of her head off the blanket like a seesaw.

"Enough?" I said.

"I think I heard hoofs."

"Deer?"

"Yes, Honey?"

"No-no. Deer as in *hoofs*." I put my ear to the blanket, heard deer hoofs. "Lay low."

Pam lay low. I lay beside her.

Gunshots rang out.

"Relax," I said.

Pam squirmed like a worm on a hook. I lay on top of her, for her protection. She kept squirming. I had a hard time relaxing, so to speak, and began squirming with her.

Soon she began screaming, along with her squirming. My kiss muzzled her screaming, and then there was only one thing to do about her squirming: have intercourse.

We did until the shots stopped, as they say. It quickly became easy to relax but then Pam began screaming again. My hand covered her mouth. Her saliva covered my palm like juice on a jar lid. I lowered my ear to the blanket, heard nothing but the sound of a pick-up shifting into second. Pam's eyes glowed like birthday candles. I took my hand off her mouth.

"ANTS!"

I put my ear closer to the blanket. "Darned quiet ones."

"On my BACK!"

I rolled off Pam, flipped her over as if she were brisket. Ants ran over her back like pioneers in cars.

"Sure enough," I said.

The ants ran lines, circles, and figure-eights. They bumped into one another, changed directions, ran faster. Most were on her neck and shoulders, but some were pushing the frontier toward the foothills.

Pam had nice foothills. She stuck her bent arm between her shoulder blades, her wrist cocked and fingers stiff, like a palsy. "They're *biting*."

Two small red ants began climbing her foothills.

"Let me get these here," I said, and I spanked the two ants away. Maybe, I thought, the honeymoon *isn't* over.

"They're worse up toward my neck," Pam said.

"Are they? Sure enough."

I tried shooing the ants off her neck. They were hard to shoo but smashed easily.

Soon eighty-seven ants lay dead on Pam's back.

"That oughta do it."

"They're still biting."

"Impossible. They're dead. Pasted."

Pam's back began growing tiny pink bumps. She put on shoes and socks and stood near the fire with the blanket around her, frowning. I went campsite to campsite, looking for Calamine.

Some of the tents were empty. Some contained people having intercourse. None had Calamine.

Beyond the tents sat a honeymoon cabin. I walked up to it. Dead moths were stuck to its front window and tiny brown puddles covered its plank-wood porch. I knocked on the door. It opened.

"Excuse me—"

I was face to face with the balloon-bellied cowboy. He wore nothing but jockey shorts with pictures of coins on them, dimes. There may have been quarters, too, but I couldn't tell, with his balloon belly hanging down like a swollen tongue.

"You still lookin' for that Polish fella?"

"I'm looking for Calamine. You got any?"

"Not in Bandera. Maybe in Pawelickville, but there ain't a single Calamine in Bandera. You need to go to Pawelickville. I'll guarantee it. Calamine. You sure that's Polish?"

Tricky Pockets

Fifty-seven miles from Pawelickville, Pam was reading her free travel brochures. I was driving.

"It's either the Pawelickville Meteor Crater or the Permian Basin Petroleum Museum," she said.

"Two nice attractions."

"Museum's only a buck to get in."

"And the crater?"

"Free."

"I vote for the crater."

"The crater it is."

I accelerated.

We found the Pawelickville Meteor Crater: a foot-deep hole the size of a parking lot. People stood in it with their arms crossed. Pam looked out her window. "What are they doing?"

"Seeing the Pawelickville Meteor Crater."

"But they're looking at the sky."

"You're right."

"They could do that at home."

"They sure could."

"Should we bother getting out?"

"Up to you."

"Ah, heck. It's free."

We got out, stepped into the crater, stood near the people, toed a few pebbles as if they were lit Salem butts.

Then Pam looked at the sky, like everyone else.

I couldn't figure out why.

I looked at the sky for the heck of it. It wasn't so bad.

"Pretty, hey?" Pam said.

I remembered her singing "Somewhere Over the Rainbow" as a child:

Blue. BIRDS. Fly . . .

"Pretty blue," I said.

"See any blue eyes around?"

The one man there old enough to be my father stood beside me, looking at the sky. His eyes were green.

I looked back at the sky. "No." I nudged the green-eyed man. "What're we looking for?"

"Meteors."

I grabbed Pam's elbow. "I think it's time we go."

We drove to downtown Pawelickville, visored our eyes with our hands like Apaches, scanning the sidewalks for a phone booth.

The Texas sun had my good used '49 Tudor running a little hot when Pam pointed. "There!"

I stopped on a dime, saw a phone booth. A man inside it opened the phone book and began tearing out pages.

"If those are the W's," I told Pam, "you're looking at your father-in-law."

Pam was still visoring her eyes.

"At ease," I said, and I got out of my good used '49 Tudor. The man in the phone booth saw me, stuffed the phone book pages into his pocket, pretended to talk into the receiver, then hung up and left the booth quickly.

"What's with the phone book pages?" I said, like a perfect stranger.

"What phone book pages?"

I looked him in the eye. "The ones in your pocket."

His eyes shifted. They were blue, like marbles. He was old enough to be my father.

"Pocket?" he said, as if pockets were a fashion that hadn't reached Pawelickville. He spoke in a shifty way, just like I'd hoped my father would. I wanted to sock him and hug him a good one.

"Your pants pocket," I said. "Right front, as I face you."

He pointed over my shoulder. "Look there!"

I kept my eyes on his pocket.

"Meteor!" he said.

I kept my eyes still. "I'll see the crater tomorrow."

This is it, I thought. I've found him. This is right up there with bluebooking with Norb Hike, marrying Pam, and my first cruise in my good used '49 Tudor.

No, I thought. This is higher.

"You're a phone company investigator," the man said. "I should have known, with all those dimes in your pocket."

"What pocket?"

"Left front, as I face you."

I looked at my pocket. It was empty, as I'd suspected.

I looked up: the man was gone.

There was a knock on the windshield of my good used '49 Tudor: Pam was bouncing on the passenger seat, pointing down main street. I jumped in my good used '49 Tudor, started it, stomped on the pedal, caught up to the man. He cut onto the sidewalk. The Tudor took the curb no problem. He raised his arms and stopped and I punched my brakes and my retreads bit the sidewalk and held.

Pam petted the dashboard. "Still a runner."

I got out, slammed the door, and approached the man from behind.

"Okay, okay," he said.

"Let's go. Out with the phone book pages."

He pulled the balled pages from his pocket, held them over his head.

I stood right behind him. "No more funny stuff."

He dropped the balled pages, which I caught like a second baseman.

"If there's W's on here . . ." I unballed the pages. "You've got some talking to do." I smoothed the pages across my thigh.

Pam got out of my good used '49 Tudor.

"B's. Nothing but gosh-darned B's. Wait. B's and a few C's. Why B's and C's?"

"Carter. I wanted Lizzy Carter's number."

"I don't see any Lizzy Carters listed here."

"Try Mary Elizabeth. It's underlined with blue ink. The pen's in my pocket."

"Never mind your pocket. Mary Elizabeth? I guess you're right. She's your girlfriend?"

"None of your business."

"You *think* so. Well think about this: ever hear of jotting a number down? You *had* a pen."

"No paper."

"Ever hear of writing on your hand?"

The man turned around. "Ever hear of palm sweat? We're in Texas, Yankee."

"Ever hear of the *back* of your hand?"

The man's blue eyes looked at me, then Pam.

"I say you're bluffing, pal," I said. "You're Seth Wirzhbinski, my smooth-talking long-lost father, and you tore out the B's and C's to throw a gooseneck in my trail. Let's go. Out with the driver's license. And no slick stuff."

Pam stepped to my side, her forehead sweating like a glass of iced tea. The man took his wallet from his back pocket, held it out at her. Her brown eyes widened, aimed at mine. I nodded. She took the wallet, pulled out the license, held it in front of her face.

"Jimmy Joe Hohman. Wrong man."

"Could've changed his name."

"No. April 3rd birthday. Your dad was born on Halloween. Gertie told me about the parties."

Hot and Cold Running Water

My speedometer read 1O7. Pam pulled a ball of blue yarn out from under the seat, measured the loose end against the length of her arm, cut it with a fingernail clippers, began tying knots in it.

"More crafts?" I asked.

She nodded.

I steered back into my lane. She kept tying knots in the blue yarn and I kept in my lane. Finally she quit tying knots, reached into a used lunch bag between her feet, took out a tiny plastic white cross, put it on the dashboard, tried punching a hole in it with the little nail file on the fingernail clippers.

"My *dash*board!"

The hole in the dashboard was smaller than the one in the cross. She tied both ends of the knotted yarn to the cross, held the works up to the windshield.

"Rosary?" I asked.

She nodded, put the rosary around her neck, measured more blue yarn against the length of her arm. "A nickel apiece."

My speedometer read 119. Something whizzed by on the right.

"What was that?" I asked.

"Hot and Cold Running Water Stand."

"For showers and Kool-Aid?"

"I'm not sure. Hang on a sec."

Pam finished tying her second rosary, put it around her neck, reached into her purse, pulled out her brochures, read three silently, began reading a fourth, then held up a finger:

"'Hot and Cold Running Water Stands are roadside stands owned by the wealthy Apache Indian Chief, Hot Running Water, and managed by his lovely Apache Indian wife, Cold Running Water.'"

"Keep going."

"'Made of adobe and strung along Arizona's highways like charms on a bracelet, these stands sell turquoise, silver, polished agates, Indian arrowheads, Arizona desert fossils, and used cars.'"

"USED CARS?"

"You wanna see the brochure?"

"No, thanks. Just the next Hot and Cold Running Water Stand. Could you keep an eye out?"

Pam measured another armlength of yarn, then nodded. I drove 114 miles. Then:

"HOT AND COLD RUNNING WATER STAND!"

"Where?"

"Ahead on the right."

I hit the brakes, stopped, saw an orange and black FOR SALE sign in the rear window of a '51 Dodge Phoenix.

I got out of my good used '49 Tudor. The Phoenix had black factory paint, virgin whitewalls all the way around, four fresh goose eggs on the left side of the odometer, and a clean-as-a-cradle engine.

Arizona Phoenix, I thought. I buried Lincoln's head in the tread, whistled to myself, heard a voice:

"You look with eye to buy?"

I looked up. An old, acorn-colored man stood staring at me: black hair braided like egg bread, no shirt, muscled arms crossed, army fatigue pants, bare feet.

"You must be Hot Running Water."

His left biceps twitched. "You must not hear me. You look with eye to buy?"

I gave him the blank stare. "Depends on the price."

"Make offer."

Pam walked into the nearby Hot and Cold Running Water Stand, a silver, rounded-off-at-the-edges mobile home.

"Three sixty-five," I said.

Hot Running Water's mouth angled down at the corners like an unused staple.

"Thing looks like it's been sitting for years," I said.

"Wrong. Hot Running Water drive this runner nowhere but mile there and back to church every Sunday since day one."

"Impossible. The odometer reads twenty-seven miles."

"Hot Running Water drive in reverse."

"Three ninety-five. Tops. And you can cut out that phony accent."

"Me? You the one who talk with rattlesnake tongue. You remind me of paleface who stop here two weeks ago. Make exact same offer you did. Looked like you, too. But older. Old enough to be your father. You have family in cahoots?"

"Not at all, Chief. The only family I have is the wife. Besides that I've got nothing but a nose for a good used car. Know what I'm saying?"

Hot Running Water stared at me.

"Now what's this about the other paleface?"

"Other paleface many desert rainfalls old. Eyes color of mountain stream, like you. Drove good runner, like you. Had good-looking squaw with him, like you. Runner and squaw many moons older than yours, though. But both in darn good shape, considering. Now don't tell Hot Running Water you and older paleface not in family cahoots."

"No family cahoots but what happens between the little lady and me behind closed doors."

Pam came out of the trailer, walked over, took off one of her rosaries, put it around Hot Running Water's neck, gave his left biceps a little squeeze. "Your arms are so *hard*!"

Hot Running Water smiled. His smile was shaped like the side of a canoe, but smaller.

I folded my arms, squeezed my own biceps, which were soft as boiled perch.

Pam pulled something out of her blouse: an arrowhead necklace. "How much?"

Hot Running Water shook his head. "For you, free."

"If it's the same to you, Chief," I said, "which way did the old paleface head?"

"Nevada."

Blood rushed through my chest like hot running water. "Vegas?"

"Yeah."

"You remember what he was driving?"

"'31 Ford Model T. Green with cream interior. Upholstery a little rough. Rubber a little thin. But good runner. Run like wind across desert."

Pam beat me into my good used '49 Tudor. I closed my door. Hot Running Water walked up to the driver's side window, studied the toilet paper rosebuds in the back seat.

I rolled down my window. "You say he passed through here two weeks ago?"

Hot Running Water nodded. "I still say you in family cahoots."

"You're sharp, Chief. But wrong. Anyway, I owe you one. For the scoop."

I turned my ignition key, revved the engine extra loud for Hot Running Water.

He flashed his canoe smile and nodded. "Purrs like bobcat. What year this baby—forty-eight?"

"Forty-nine. Good guess, though."

"Hot Running Water have nose for good used car, too."

I began rolling up my window. "You don't really talk that way, do you, old timer?"

Hot Running Water didn't answer. My wheels began rolling and he cupped his hand around his mouth:

"YOU AND YOUR OLD MAN WANNA OPEN ONE OF THESE STANDS IN VEGAS? I'M THINKING OF STARTING A FRANCHISE."

My tires squealed.

Too Many
Scottie Dogs

My good used '49 Tudor crossed the Exotic Nevada border. Pam sat erect in the passenger seat with her arrowhead necklace and her first fifty rosaries around her neck. Her used purse sat on her lap. She lifted her chin. "Green Ford!"

"That's a Chrysler."

"Sorry."

I felt tingling on the corner of my mouth, so I touched it while I drove with one hand.

"Cold sore?" Pam said.

"Fever blister."

"Gertie told me your father used to get those all the time."

"That's another lead."

"Blue eyes, a green '31 Model T, and now cold sores."

"*Fev*er blisters."

"Fever blisters."

I touched the tingling. "Now if I could just get rid of mine."

"Hang on." Pam stuck her arm in her purse, dug around, covered the dashboard with expired coupons, restaurant salt shakers, a chain of barrettes, tangled brown hair, used travel brochures.

I quit touching the tingling and watched the road, driving with both hands.

Pam kept digging. "Ah."

I gave her a glance. Something like a thick yellow button sat on her cupped palm.

"That a doorknob?"

"Don't be silly."

"Breath mint?"

"No. Lip balm. Supposed to cure fever blisters. Carmex, they call it."

"Cures fever blisters?"

Pam unscrewed the yellow cap. "*And* cold sores."

I smeared a fingertip of Carmex on the tingling.

"Cover the whole lip," she said. "For protection."

Covering my whole lip felt like fingerpainting a cocktail sausage. "A pleasant enough scent."

"They make it in Wisconsin," Pam said. She squinted at the tiny black words on the yellow cap. "In Franklin."

"You sure are something. Kiss?"

"Kiss."

Pam and I kissed. I drove 134 miles. Las Vegas rose from the horizon like biscuits. Pam looked at me and frowned. "Those are cold sores."

I pulled over, gave my lip a good look in the rear-view mirror. Cold sores were lined up along the top of my lip like 3P women stuffing used purses in a buffet line. I looked at Pam. She was touching the two lines that connected her nostrils and upper lip.

"Tingling?" I asked.

She nodded.

"Maybe it's an omen. A dime to a Coke that before sunset we see a middle-aged, blue-eyed man with fever blisters."

"*Cold* sores."

"Whatever."

Pam reached inside her purse. "You never know." She pulled out her little yellow jar, covered her whole lip with Carmex.

We rolled into Vegas. Pam kept fingering those ridges.

"Cold sore?" I asked.

She nodded.

I drove two miles, pulled over, gave her cold sore a good look. It was shaped like Ohio. Her eyes glistened like two Great Lakes. I looked at Las Vegas. "I hear cold sores are good luck."

Pam tried to smile.

"How much in the kitty?" I asked.

The kitty was in the dashboard ashtray, more coins than bills.

"Seventy-two something."

I grabbed a tenspot from the kitty, one of those old velvety ones. "We'll bet this into thousands. Then we'll travel like Rockefellers until we find my long-lost father. When it's all said and done, we'll look back on these cold sores and laugh."

"I'd like to see Saskatchewan."

We drove down the Strip, parked in a lot two blocks over. Some good runners were parked there, but no green '31 Model T's. We got out of my good used '49 Ford Tudor and walked to the Strip, where people came at us like buffaloes.

"Crowded as St. Josie's bazaar," Pam said. She took a few rosaries off her neck, looped them around her forearm, held them out at people walking by. "Rosaries," she shouted. "Three for a quarter."

"Watch for those blue eyes and cold sores," I said. "I feel lucky."

A man with blue eyes came at us and walked past, acting invisible. He was old enough to be my father.

"No cold sores," Pam said.

I stopped, turned, and cupped my hands around my mouth: "WIRZHBINSKI!"

The man kept walking.

Pam had kept walking also, opposite the man. I ran a few steps, caught up with her. "What's the hurry?"

She pointed ahead. A man with silver hair around a bald-spot the size of a beverage coaster was walking arm-in-arm with a woman old enough to be my mother. She was small-boned, with an egg timer figure. A rhinestone evening dress hung from her shoulders, a rhinestone purse from her hand.

Pam kept pointing at the man. "Cold sores."

"On the *bald*spot?"

"Of course not. On the corners of his mouth. He walked out of the casino back there when you yelled Wirzhbinski. He gave you a nervous look, caught me looking at his cold sores and started walking."

"And the woman?"

"No cold sores."

"But nice-looking besides that?"

"For her age."

Pam and I walked faster, caught up with the baldspot and rhinestones. I tapped the man on the shoulder. He stopped, turned, and put his hand over his mouth, as if coughing. His eyes were blue and didn't act the cough out, and the black pores on his nose said he was old enough to be my father.

This is it, I thought.

I reached for the hand over his mouth. "Let's see those cold sores."

I saw rhinestones, purple and yellow stars, then nothing but black.

When I came to I was lying on the carpeted foyer of a casino, my head propped by Pam's shoes. I could tell they were her shoes without looking because her feet have this dirty, sexy smell.

Then I looked up. Pam stood beside me in her stocking feet, pulling the chain of her arrowhead necklace through the tiny hole in the arrowhead, talking to a slick-haired Italian kid in a red valet outfit. There were ice cubes in his hand. He looked at me. "Those are just cold sores," Pam told him.

I sat up. A headache hit me like a sucker punch. Pam turned, stooped down beside me like a stuck Russian dancer, gave the Italian kid the high sign. "Thanks anyway."

The Italian kid smirked and walked away.

"Thanks for *what*," I said.

Pam looked at the black and white patterned carpeting. I did also. The pattern was little black and white Scottie dogs.

"For dragging you in here," she said.

The Scottie dogs were in rows: black, white, black, white—hundreds of Scottie dogs. Looking at them made my head throb, so I looked at Pam. "How long was I out?"

"Ten minutes. Mrs. Rhinestone connected with her clutch purse."

I touched the corner of my mouth, held my finger in front of my eyes. "Cut?"

"Bloody cold sores."

"What about the guy with the blue eyes and cold sores?"

"Not your father. This guy was some sort of ambassador."

"You sure?"

"He showed me papers."

"Couldn't my father be an ambassador?"

"Not this ambassador. This guy couldn't speak English."

"Maybe he was bluffing."

"I called him a son of a bitch three times. He didn't flinch once."

I grabbed Pam's small hand. "Let's hit the crap table."

She grabbed my soft biceps. "Craps we can shoot at home. Let's try them fruit things." She pulled me across a thousand or so Scottie dogs to the far corner of the casino. A man sat behind a window of gold bars like a speechless parakeet. He chewed gum as if it contained oxygen.

"Ten dollars in nickels," Pam said.

The man kept chewing his gum, nodded, and slid a paper cup of nickels under the gold bars. Pam grabbed it and I tapped her shoulder. "You done this before?"

She shook her head, grabbed my sleeve with her free hand, led me back across more Scottie dogs to some slot machines near the foyer. "The ones near the entrance spit the most jackpots."

"Your friend Vito tell you that?"

"Shh."

I turned, looked at the end of the slot machine row. The Italian kid stood looking away, smirking.

I stepped beside Pam, held a cocktail napkin to my bleeding cold sores with one hand, the cup of nickels in the other. She pumped nickel after nickel into a slot machine, which acted more like a closed fire hydrant.

Ten minutes later we were in an all-night restaurant, sitting at a table the size of a chessboard, sharing a nineteen cent pancake-and-egg breakfast.

Pam poured artificial maple syrup on our silver dollar pancakes. She watched her syrup run off the edges, then drip.

"So much for Saskatchewan," she said.

Returning

My good used '49 Tudor was headed east. Pam was counting the kitty. "You shouldn't have played that dumb roulette wheel," she said. "This won't even get us to Omaha."

I accelerated. "Maybe a trucker'll buy your stupid rosaries."

She gave me her dirtiest look, then scooted up against the passenger door.

I drove a few miles. We passed an abandoned car. "Stop at the next gas station," Pam said.

"You need to *potty* again?"

"Just stop at the next gas station."

A gas station approached. Pam pointed at it and tugged on her arrowhead necklace. I pulled over and stopped. She got out of the car, took a dime from the kitty, and headed for the phone booth.

I rolled down my window. "I THOUGHT WE WERE SUPPOSED TO BE *SAVING* MONEY."

She walked faster, made a phone call, got back in my good used '49 Tudor, sat as far away from me as possible.

"Any Wirzhbinskis?"

"Of course not. Drive back to that abandoned car."

"Why."

"Just drive."

I laid down some rubber, drove back to the abandoned car, pulled over. Pam dug into the seat crevice behind me, found a pen, took a used envelope out of her purse, slapped it on the dashboard. She pointed the pen at the abandoned car. "That a Chevy?"

I nodded.

She wrote on the envelope, neat but quickly:

CHEVY TITLE

We sat without speaking for awhile. Then a tow truck pulled up behind us. Pam folded the envelope, stuffed it between her breasts, handed me her fingernail clippers. "When he slides underneath to hook her up, cut the dash wire to his radio." She got out of my good used '49 Tudor. So did I. We walked over to the tow truck. The driver was bug-eyed, had an Adam's apple the size of a hand ball, smelled like road tar, and smiled at Pam. She nodded at the abandoned Chevy. "Take 'er away."

He maneuvered his tow truck behind the Chevy, got out, and started hooking things up. When he slid under the Chevy, I opened the tow truck door and clipped the rainbow of wires between his radio and dash. He slid out from under the Chevy, stood, and smiled at Pam. "Got the cash, ma'am?"

"Cash?" Pam said. She undid her top blouse button.

His Adam's apple bobbed. "Our policy is you pay up front. Didn't my dispatcher tell you?"

She fingered the next button down. "Didn't your dispatcher tell you about the deal?"

His eyes were bugging so much I couldn't stand it.

"Your dispatcher's buying the car," Pam told him. She slid a scissors of fingers into her left bra cup, took the envelope from between her breasts. The driver swallowed so hard I heard it. Pam held the words "CHEVY TITLE" in front of his face and shoved the envelope into his shirt pocket. "Everything's signed," she said. "Just give me the twenty. Your dispatcher said take it out of your cash pouch."

The driver's eyes seemed stuck open. "I'll have to call my dispatcher." He got in his tow truck for awhile, came back out, looked at Pam. "Radio don't work."

"How 'bout you?" Pam asked him. "Interested? Ten bucks and it's yours."

He looked at Pam's blouse button, then the abandoned Chevy.

"Turn around and sell it to your dispatcher for the twenty," she said. "If he changes his mind, you got a hundred dollars worth a parts for ten."

He blinked a few times.

"Shocks are less than a week old," Pam said.

I decided to help out. "Got it all hooked up," I said.

The driver dug into his back pocket, gave Pam a crumpled ten. "Why not."

We got in my good used '49 Tudor. Pam crammed the ten into the ashtray. "On to Omaha," she said.

I started my good used '49 Tudor, turned the tow truck into a toy miniature in my rear-view. Pam and I didn't look at each other for sixteen miles. Then I spied on her out of the corner of my eye. She sat staring ahead proudly, as if she'd just sold an oil well. I drove another mile, glanced at the tenspot, then felt my face soften and smile.

Squirrels

I wiped my dipstick with my handkerchief. The gas station attendant was pumping her full. "Look how red it is," Pam said.

"You should see the ones across the river," the gas station attendant told her. "Black as shoe polish."

I stabbed my dipstick into the little hole and noticed that Pam was pointing at a red squirrel hopping across the gas station driveway.

"Which river," she asked the gas station attendant.

He smiled. I thought: For the rest of my life men will be wanting to kiss Pam. I wasn't sure I liked that. "The Missouri," he said. "Drive over the I-29 bridge and you'll see them. Black squirrels, everywhere. And not a one here in Omaha."

I started my good used '49 Tudor, paid the guy two dollars. "That the bridge east to Council Bluffs?"

He began pushing buttons on his silver changer. "Yeah. Course there ain't any red squirrels on their side . . ." He kept pushing buttons. "So . . ." He dropped the change on my palm. "So it all evens out." We both stared at the change. "It all evens out! GET IT?"

I drove off. My good used '49 Tudor began crossing the I-29 bridge. Pam looked at the Missouri River and said, "Squirrels must not swim good."

I dropped the change into the kitty. "What're we down to."

"Seventy-four cents."

"I guess we just drive and starve."

"Or try one of my dad's old tricks."

I raised my eyebrows.

"Pull into that apple orchard."

I pulled into the only apple orchard I saw: a red barn beside rows of trees with bad posture and people between them. Men stood holding wooden poles with coffee cans on their ends and pieces of rope hanging down. Women pointed at the highest apples. Kids jumped at low branches like dancing poodles.

I cut the engine. "A guy almost wants to get out and join 'em."

"Not today," Pam said.

Then she had me lie in the back seat without moving or making a sound. She sat in the driver's seat. The sun began sinking. She stuck her arm out the window and waved.

"Who you waving at?"

"The orchardman."

I sat up. "Is that necessary?"

"Lay down. Ah, don't bother. He went back in."

I looked out the windshield. Men were returning from the trees carrying lumpy grocery bags. Pam took off her rosaries, threw them on my lap, got out of my good used '49 Tudor.

"What's going on here?" I said.

"Trust me."

I began getting out of the back seat and she closed the door against my knee.

"Stay in the car."

"*Oh* no."

"Okay already. But don't let him see you."

She led me to the red barn, stopped at the open barn door. I stood behind her. Inside the barn was the orchardman, the men, the women, the kids, lumpy grocery bags, a scale, an apple-squeezing machine, a pyramid of ten bottles of cider, and about 257 boxes of apples. The kids were pointing at the apple-squeezing machine, eyes big as bottle caps. The men and women stood in line in front of the scale, arms crossed, lumpy grocery bags at their feet.

The line shrunk. The barn grew darker. People left until there was one man, one woman, and a kid who wouldn't keep still. The man put the bag on the scale. The woman took an apple tree twig to the rotten apple meat on the kid's shoes.

"Wait here," Pam said, and she approached the orchardman. The orchardman saw her. My knees quivered like poisoned rats. Pam inhaled through her nose, winked at the orchardman. "Smells like a ripe crop. Mind if I clear away a few fallens?"

The orchardman winked back. "Not at all." Winking again, he didn't see me in his barn door. Pam turned, headed toward me, and walked past as if she hadn't seen me either. I tried to follow. Night was black. Marriage, I thought.

I heard Pam giggle. "*Hurry.* Before he comes looking. You know those orchardmen."

We ran toward the trees, barely saw our first Council Bluffs, Iowa, squirrel: the thing was so black I almost kicked it.

Soon fallen apples filled the trunk of my good used '49 Tudor like so many sticks of butter, and I was pulling out of the orchard driveway. "You hear him looking for you in that next row over? What did he call you—his little golden delicious?"

"Fun, hey?" Pam said.

"Didn't cost nothin'."

"And totally honest. Let's drive up those bluffs so's we can eat."

"And sleep."

Pam grinned in the blue glow of the dashboard.

Loose Connection

Something squeaked like a bad front end. I lifted my head, banged it against the steering wheel, and opened my eyes. "Christ," I whispered, and I rubbed the growing bump near my hairline.

Two cardinals red as match heads were squeaking and flitting through the ditchweed between my windshield and the bluff. A Council Bluffs, Iowa, squirrel sat watching them: black. I turned around. Pam lay on the back seat, curled asleep on a bed of toilet paper rosebuds, head propped on the armrest, a string of drool connecting her open mouth to the upholstery like five inches of fishline.

"Morning, gorgeous," I said.

Her eyes stayed closed. "Apples." Her mouth stayed open.

I grabbed the steering wheel, watched the ditchweed and our kitty turn green in the morning sun.

I had more than a man could ask for: Norb Hike's daughter as a wife and a good low-mileage runner.

I did not need to find my long lost father.

I needed to get home and sell used cars.

Pam woke, put four fallen apples in the styrofoam cooler, took the jackhandle from the trunk, and made applesauce.

We ate the applesauce.

Then we decided to clean up:

"Your jackhandle's sticky."

"Just throw it in the trunk—Here, I'll do it."

My good used '49 Ford Tudor started. We began our last day of driving. Suddenly my good used '49 Tudor began bucking, knocking, and grinding, like silverware in a running garbage disposal.

I turned to Pam, watched the sounds of twisting metal wipe twenty-two days of honeymoon happiness from her face.

Then I cut the ignition.

She fingered one of the knots on a rosary around her neck. "What was *that*?"

"Don't even ask."

I stepped out of the car and raised the hood.

Then I closed the hood.

The smell of a dead car is worse than that of human flesh.

Pam came to my side. "Thrown rod?" she said, with caution, grace and timing. She was truly her father's daughter, and I loved her for that.

We got in the back seat and I showed her my love three times, like a mink.

Then I said, "Thank God we're on an upgrade."

I got out of the back seat, raised the hood, and disconnected the coil wire. Pam watched from the other side of the open hood. "Why the coil wire?"

"So she won't start. That way we can sell her without the buyer hearing the engine."

"And if the buyer sees it's the coil wire?"

"Even better. He'll think she's one turn of the screw from running. He'll think he's taking us. That's exactly what you want your buyer thinking."

We got in the front seat. I threw the car in neutral and we coasted backwards to Abel's Used Cars, on the outskirts of Council Bluffs.

Abel's Used Cars was forty-four good runners surrounding a log cabin of an office. A pot-bellied man in a gray beard and mirrored glasses sat on the cabin porch steps, twisting his beard as if beard-twisting paid bills. He wore baggy corduroy pants, suspenders, a plaid flannel shirt over a dingy V-neck. A baggie of cashews sat between his steel-tipped boots.

This'll be easy, I thought. Pam and I approached him like lost dogs after a thunderstorm. He chewed cashews as if we weren't there.

"Know much about cars besides selling 'em?" I said.

He cocked his head in my general direction. "Only by feel, son. Lost my eyes ten years ago, cleaning gunk from the gas tank of a '44 Chrysler. But that don't mean I can't help you."

The blind used car dealer trick was nothing new to me.

Or Pam.

She looked at me and I nodded.

I kept an eye out for passersby and she yanked her stretch-pants down past her knees.

The man kept chewing cashews.

I gave him the old fake-kick-to-the-face, just to make sure. He kept chewing. Pam pulled up her pants. My ears tingled. "You really *are* blind," I said.

"Speak up, Son," he said. "Deaf in one ear, too."

"I'm sorry," I said, louder.

"Don't pity me. You're the one with car problems."

"How'd you know I had problems?"

"Didn't hear no engine. Either you got car problems or you came on horseback, in which case you wouldn't be here."

Pam's lower lip curled over itself.

"So what's wrong with it?" the man said.

"Nothing serious," I said, winking at Pam. "The car's a runner. But I woke up this morning after camping up in the bluffs with the wife here, and she just wouldn't start. The car, I mean."

The man pushed his sunglasses into the red notch on his nose.

"I was wondering if you'd take it in a trade for something that's running here. So we can get to Wisconsin before sundown."

The man stopped chewing. "Wis*con*sin." He began twisting his beard again. "What's in Wisconsin that can't wait a few days?"

It took me a second longer than normal to answer. All this long-lost father stuff had me out of shape haggling-wise.

"Family reunion," I said. "We're coming from Colorado."

"Interesting. You wouldn't be trying to con a helpless blind man, would you?"

"You think I'd run a '49 Tudor all the way from Colorado just to play car dealer?"

"You say *Tudor*?"

"A '49. Right after the war."

"And you say its guts are clean?"

"Transmission, brakes, front end—all A-1. Everything but a bug keeping her from starting. A bug I don't have time to find."

"How 'bout the engine."

I elbowed Pam. "Purrs like a bobcat."

"Hmmm. Mind if I feel her over?"

"Hood's already popped." I walked to my '49 Tudor.

The man didn't move. I winked at Pam. She took his hand, led him over. His hands ran wild over the body: the car's.

"It's a Tudor all right. Feels pretty smooth."

He began feeling under the hood. His fingers touched the loose coil wire, hesitated, kept moving. I nudged Pam. She smiled. The man kept feeling: upholstery, dashboard, floorboard, tire tread, muffler. When his hands stopped, his mouth opened:

"Couldn't offer you much. After all, we don't know why she ain't startin'."

"You gotta admit she felt clean."

"For her age. But she's decades old. And remember, I can't see the paint. What color is she, anyway?"

"Red," I said, for good measure.

Pam hid a giggle.

The man twisted his beard. "I'll trade you that '52 Chevy, straight up. As is for as is."

He held out a set of keys, pointed in the general direction of a bondoed '52 Belair.

Pam took the keys and started the Belair. It missed a little but didn't choke out.

"Mind if I talk it over with the wife?"

"Go right ahead."

Pam and I huddled.

"You're Norb Hike's daughter. Think it'll make it?"

She looked me in the eye. "When you're trading away a thrown rod, *any*thing's a runner."

The man and I signed over the titles.

Within minutes I was driving my good used '52 Belair beneath Iowa's bluest sky ever. Pam was gazing out the passenger window at the rows of feed corn.

"The kitty," she said.

"You don't have it? I checked the ashtray before I signed the title. I thought you'd already taken it."

"I checked the ashtray *while* you signed the title. I thought *you'd* taken it."

I braked, did a U-turn, charged back toward Council Bluffs like a rhinoceros, pulled onto the lot with a screech. Mr. Beard had his head under the hood of the '49 Tudor. Both of his hands were behind his back, but I didn't make much of that then.

I stepped out of my '52 Chevy Belair.

He turned and faced me. "You conned me, you son-of-a-bitch."

"You stole my kitty, bastard."

Suddenly I realized that his mirrored glasses were in the

pocket of his flannel shirt, that he was looking at me with the bluest of eyes, and that there was a cold sore hidden behind the grizzle of his beard.

And there was no question: he was old enough to be my father.

"It's *you*," I said. "Of course it's you. Who else could have fooled me with the blind dealer trick?"

He pulled his mirrored glasses from his pocket, put them on. "I don't know what you're talking about."

"You're Seth Wirzhbinski. You scammed me just as you were scammed years ago, right before you skipped town, leaving me at the mercy of my penny-pinching grandparents on the South Side of Milwaukee."

The man twisted his beard and looked at Pam for a long time. She smiled. He smiled back, then looked me in the eye.

"My son," he said.

We hugged like magnet to metal.

My tight throat barricaded words until I whispered a word I had never before spoken:

"Pop."

We pressed chests, slapped backs, did our best to fight tears.

"My son. My son. Who else could have sold me a thrown rod?"

The Hole

According to my father, there were five ways to use the term "son of a bitch."

Most common was "son-of-a-bitch." Meaning *scoundrel.*

Another was "*son* of a bitch." Meaning *darn* or *damn.*

There's also "you son-of-a-*bitch*, you." Words of envy or admiration.

Then there's "*Son. Of. A. Bitch.*" An expression of pleasant surprise, often spoken by used car men running into each other unexpectedly—in a drugstore, for instance.

And of course there's the old "son-of-a-BITCH." A used car man's version of "ouch."

My father explained this to me in his Council Bluffs car lot cabin, the Sunday morning after our reunion.

We were sitting at his kitchen table, eating breakfast. Pam was still on the porch couch, sleeping. My father poured syrup on his bare plate until it looked like a rusty ice rink, covered the syrup with four pancakes, two sausage patties and a can of mandarin oranges, and forked himself a mouthful.

I did the same thing.

He slurped down a Kerr jar of coffee the color of Pepsi.

A full Kerr jar sat beside my plate. I'd never drunk coffee before. I lifted it to my lips, and my father began icing his pile with more syrup and said, "I suppose you wanna know why I flew the coop."

I glanced over my shoulder at the porch. I couldn't see Pam, or hear stirring. "I've heard rumors."

"All the more reason to know the truth."

I sipped some coffee.

My father finished icing his pile, began cutting it with his fork. "How much you know about Johnny Casanova?"

"You mean Liquid Johnny?"

"Yeah."

"I know he's a smooth-talking *son* of a bitch who reads people like headlines and does well with cars on account of it."

This was when my father gave me the word on the whole "son of a bitch" thing.

"Liquid isn't a *son* of a bitch," he explained. "He's a son-of-a-bitch."

I nodded.

He stuffed a forkful of his pile into his mouth. Mandarin orange juice dripped off his beard. "You never heard about the mob connection?"

"Not really."

He glanced over his shoulder at the porch. "When I left Milwaukee, Liquid was making most of his money on the public end of a stolen car racket. Hike never told you about this?"

I put my Kerr jar near my lips, shook my head.

"A guy third in command in Chicago named Tar Face Marconi used to run stolen cars up from Florida." He held his fork as if it were a three-on-the-tree gearshift, and cut hard into his pile. "And store them in a warehouse Liquid owned south of town."

"Near Kenosha?"

"You seen it?"

"I *lived* there. On the Kenosha property, I mean. I never saw the warehouse."

"The warehouse was two miles deep in elm trees. An easy warehouse to miss—"

"Was it scorched? A Quonset hut?"

"Come to think of it, yeah."

"I *have* seen it."

"You see what was going on inside?"

"No."

"This Marconi had some kid pull the engines and paint the cars over. Kid stayed in an old farmhouse there. With a collie."

"*I* lived in that farmhouse. With a deaf guy named Mike and a German shepherd."

"Same guy. Collie must have run off or something. Dogs do that, you know."

"Dogs and fathers."

My father nodded, stabbed his fork into his pile, and began twisting his beard. "Marconi and his people would run these cars up from Florida and lift the engines. And these were good engines—Marconi ran nothing but next-to-new cars. They'd lift them and sell them as rebuilts through a shop Liquid owned. On Kinnickinnic Avenue."

"A-1 Engines?"

"The son-of-a-bitch still owns it?"

"Yeah, but he talks like it's losing him money."

"Of course he does. He's gotta keep things under cover. But that's just the half of it. When I was there, Liquid would sell the painted-over bodies on his lot—after the deaf kid put burnt-out engines in 'em."

"Engines customers brought in to A-1 Engines?"

"Right. Then he and Marconi split everything sixty-forty, with Marconi getting the fat half."

"And I thought he bought cheap because he read people so well. Norb Hike told me that."

"Now that ain't exactly hot air. There was a time when Liquid read faces like directions on sparkler boxes, and made out well doing it. Matter of fact that's how he got connected with Marconi in the first place. Met him in a special ticket window line at Sportsman's. Saw mob in Marconi's eyes from moment one. An hour later, he had his connection."

"Sparkler boxes," I said.

My father didn't answer, just ate his pile as quietly as a used car man could. Then he pushed away from the table and walked over to the sink.

He returned with an open box of toothpicks. "Lumber?"

"Sure."

Pam walked in, smiled at my father, rubbed her eyes with her knuckles, and yawned. She looked Chinese. "You know you got a sinkhole out back?"

My father's toothpick fell from his mouth.

"Not funny," I said.

"But true," Pam said. "Thing just swallowed a stack of used tires."

My father, Pam and I ran out back, then stared at the sinkhole. It was two and a half feet wide: a donut hole in the earth's crust eating its way into babka-sized proportions like an ulcer. I'd never seen a sinkhole before, and this one had used tires in it.

"Tires weren't worth much," my father said. "But we gotta stop that hole."

The Mistake

As it turned out, my father had never been to Arizona.

He'd never owned a green '31 Model T with a cream interior, either.

And he'd never spent time with an older, nice-looking woman.

Hot Running Water had had me guessing all wrong.

Since leaving Milwaukee, my father had always lived in his log cabin office with his refrigerator, Army surplus cot, and five gallon pail of wholesale cashews.

"He don't need us here," Pam told me the third morning we'd been there. She was sitting on my father's cot making toilet paper rosebuds—yellow ones. "He's used to being on his own. He don't like me."

My father was outside, pushing a '47 Thunderbird on an alderman.

"Not true," I said. "That sinkhole's just getting to him. In fact he thinks you're the cat's meow. He wants us all to move to an apricot farm in Montana. Grow 'cots and fish trout streams. Keep a few runners around for scratch money. Drive to At-Ok-Ad now and then and play the ponies. The good life."

"What's At-Ok-Ad?"

"Dakota spelled backwards. Name of a racetrack up there."

"Sounds pretty ritzy. I hope your dad can afford the apricot farm. We only got eighty-six cents in the kitty."

"He can't. But I got an idea."

My father walked in without the alderman. The '47 Thunderbird sat on the lot, hood open. My father puffed his cheeks, let them deflate like two hairy balloons, headed for his cashew pail. "Saw the darned gasket leak."

"Damn politicians," Pam said.

Opening the pail, my father talked over his shoulder: "And that sinkhole ain't getting any smaller."

Pam grabbed a used bread bag tie. "Nothing you can do about that."

My father filled his used baggie with cashews, threw one in his mouth, and stepped beside me, chewing.

I rubbed my jaw. "You two think you can manage a few days by yourselves here?"

Pam finished a yellow rosebud, looked my father square in the eye. He stopped chewing cashews. They smiled at each other.

"Sure," she said, and she faced me. "Why?"

I tugged at my longest chin whisker. "I'm going back to Milwaukee."

The Link

I put 497 miles on one of my father's used cars: a '52 Volkswagen with a broken speedometer but a hole in the floorboard that gave a good enough estimate to get me to Kenosha safely.

I pulled onto Norb Hike's property. The Volks choked out in the driveway. Beside the worm farm lay a giant cylinder the color of old paper. Norb Hike was crawling on the farm, throwing wet cardboard everywhere, his ass-crack winking over the top of his trousers like the eye of a toy Santa.

I got out of the car. "No dome yet?" I asked the crack.

Norb Hike turned around, dropped a piece of cardboard, blinked hard.

"Hey-hey," I said.

His eyes and mouth opened wide. "*Son. Of. A. Bitch.* I thought yous were gone for good."

"*Oh* no."

He stood on some mud chunks, crammed his hands into his pockets, jingled some spare change. "Honeymoon's over?"

"Heck yeah."

He pointed at the giant cylinder. I thought it was used linoleum. "Wanna help roll this out?" he asked.

"Sure."

We unrolled 1,600 square feet of used lavender carpeting over wet mud. Now Norb Hike's worm farm had cigarette burns and beer stains.

"Carpeted worm farm," I said. "Pretty fancy."

"Really brings 'em up. Alls I gotta do to get my daily gross is roll back a corner."

"Beats the heck out of cardboard."

"And how. Where's your better half?"

I pictured Pam and my father eating *golumpkas* on my father's porch, then tried not to picture what my mother did with Liquid Johnny. "That's what I'm here to talk about. How'd you like your own used car lot?"

The Sauce

There's a business no one knows about: stamp-soaking.

Stamp-soaking involves searching trash dumpsters for used envelopes, steaming the stamps free, soaking the postmarks off with a secret solution, and selling the stamps at half their face value.

I discovered stamp-soaking when I visited the Chicago mob's third-in-command man, Tar Face Marconi.

Tar Face Marconi had never soaked a single stamp in his life, but he lived with his mother and she soaked stamps as if her heartbeat depended on it.

"I'm out of stamps. Where's Mamma Tar Face?"

"I wanna send this teddy to a dame in Kansas City. Where's Mamma Tar Face?"

"I hate standing in line by these FBI posters. Where's Mamma Tar Face?"

Mamma Tar Face lived in the middle of a bad-smelling block of Chicago bungalows. I saw her only once, the day after I helped carpet Norb Hike's worm farm.

I knocked on the bungalow's front door whiffing the bad smell. The door opened to a man wearing a sharkskin suit, silk socks, a napkin hanging from his collar, and orange meatsauce on his chin. A woman in a yellow dress stood on her hands and knees behind him: face red, hair gray, cantaloupe-sized calves, veins thick as nightcrawlers. Hundreds of three cent stamps covered damp newspaper sections spread all over the floor.

"Wrong address," the man said, and he slammed the door on my shoetips.

I knocked again, kept knocking. The door opened. The

man, newspaper sections and stamps were gone. The woman stood behind the door, on her feet, looking at me like St. Cecilia.

"Yes?"

I smelled wet newsprint. "Your son home?"

"My son don't a live here. He lives in a motels in Indiana. He's a traveling greeting a card a salesman and his a sales route is the northern a half of Indiana. If you don't a believe me, talk to my a lawyer."

"Don't worry, ma'am. I'm no G-man. I'm a friend of Liquid Johnny's. I'm here to make an offer."

The woman slammed the door on my shoetips.

I knocked again, so many times I had to change knuckles. Three knuckles later the door opened. The man stood there, this time in a seersucker suit, crew socks and leather sandals. He still had the meatsauce on his chin and the stock gangster complexion: pockmarks.

Tar Face Marconi, I thought. His face actually looked more like old asphalt than tar, but I wasn't there to quibble.

"Mr. Marconi?"

"Let's see your piece."

"Piece?"

"Yeah. *Piece.*"

"Oh. I don't carry a piece."

"No piece? How bout a name—you got one of those?"

I gave the question all it deserved: a thought. "Call me Knuckles," I said.

He gave me a long, tough look. The meatsauce on his chin made that difficult. "Mr. Knuckles. What can you do for me?"

"Make you some money."

"I quit the racecourse three days ago. For good. Damn photos are bad on the ticker."

"I'm not talking ponies. I'm talking sure money."

"What kind of sure money you talking?"

"Used cars."

Tar Face Marconi's face went white as concrete. "You got the wrong Marconi."

I took a long look at a pockmark. "I don't think so. I happen to know a man who owes you a lot of money and wants to clear his name."

"That Polack? Wurstshooski?"

I nodded. "Wirzhbinski."

"We searched *Ca*nada for that throat snot. Couldn't find

his name in a single phone book. Where is he?"

"That's my secret. And it'll stay mine if you want your money back. You think we could discuss this inside? Darn smell out here is starting to get me. Your trashmen on strike?"

He pointed down the block. "Yeast factory." He looked over his shoulder. The woman stood in the middle of the living room, wiping her hands on her yellow dress. She nodded.

"Be my guest," Tar Face Marconi said.

I walked past him.

"Mamma? Knuckles."

Mamma Tar Face stared at Tar Face like he was crazy. I sat on a black leather couch. She lugged her calves and varicose veins in front of Tar Face, grabbed his jaw with one hand, licked the thumb of the other and rubbed the meatsauce off his chin.

Tar Face rolled his eyes.

She licked her thumb again, rubbed his chin harder, slapped his face gently, walked out of the room. I looked at the floor. He cleared his throat, then sat next to me.

I pretended I couldn't smell what stunk: her saliva drying on his chin. "Liquid's been stiffing you on the numbers game for twenty-some years," I said.

"You think I don't know that?"

"I *know* you know that. What I don't know is if he's got something coming for that."

"Of course he's got something coming for that. That's not the question. The question is when."

"The answer is now. With a con that'll get you the dough Wirzhbinski owes you. And more."

Tar Face Marconi sniffed one armpit, then the other. "I'm listening."

"You tell Liquid Johnny the Feds are onto your car-heisting operation. Tell him your sources say the Feds are gonna make the bust on the public end."

"Liquid Yoshu's Sparkling Motors?"

"Right."

"So how does that put dough in my safe?"

"Hang on. There's more."

"Get on with it. I'm no pudding brain."

"Okay. You tell Liquid to sell the lot to dodge the heat."

"But I'm making good money out of that lot. We finally got it running smooth."

"Of course you are. So you tell Liquid you want to beat the

heat by re-routing the cars—distributing them someplace where the heat won't suspect."

"Like where?"

Something crumpled in the next room, probably newspaper. "Just tell him you're re-routing through Kansas City."

"I got nothing but enemies in Kansas City."

"Does Liquid Johnny know that?"

"No."

"Fine then. Just tell him to sell his lot to a stool pigeon in Milwaukee and buy another one near Kansas City."

"Why you so big on Kansas City?"

"The con won't work unless he buys a certain car lot near there. Which lot, I can't tell you."

"Listen, Knuckles. I don't join no con unless I can trust my partner. Which lot."

"I tell you that and I'm blowing Wirzhbinski's cover. I'm sorry, Mr. Marconi, but you're already getting screwed by one partner. If you wanna teach him a lesson and get your dough back from Wirzhbinski, you're gonna have to trust me."

Tar Face stared at me for a long time. Sweat beaded onto his clean shaven chin. Beats meatsauce, I thought.

"Trust is a dirty word in my line of work, Mr. Knuckles. I don't get involved with nothing without knowing details. Maybe I don't need to know which dealership, but I need to know details. Like exactly how this con is gonna work."

I stared at Tar Face. My chin wouldn't sweat. "All right," I said. "I happen to know that you and Liquid are yanking cherry engines from hot cars and selling them through A-1 Motors. I also happen to know that you're taking A-1's garbage engines, sticking them in the hot chasses and selling the works as next-to-new cars through Liquid Yoshu's Sparkling Motors."

"That ain't news to me."

"Fine. So you tell Liquid he needs to buy a lot near Kansas City or you'll cut him off. I arrange for him to *find* a particular lot there, one with a big inventory of clean cars and a good reputation, something he'll need to sink some dough into, say a hundred thou—uh, grand. I get him to shake on a cash-up-front deal there and tell him we need the cash in a week. He sells Liquid Yoshu's Sparkling Motors to one of my men for a prayer and a song—because the heat's supposedly on—and gets up the cash he's saved from screwing you on the numbers racket to make the K.C. purchase. Meantime I take the good engines out of the clean cars on the lot in K. C., and exchange them for garbage ones. See we're getting him on the same con you and him have been pulling on his customers for years, but on a bigger scale."

"Uh-huh."

"And I don't just yank engines. I yank transmissions, master cylinders—anything I can sell to parts dealers and he won't notice missing by eyeballing the lot. He signs and hands over the cash and he's out the hundred grand."

"How you gonna get him to sign and pay without looking at the guts of the cars?"

"That's my business."

"And then I get the hundred g-notes?"

"You get twenty. That's what Wirzhbinski owes you, isn't it?"

"There's been interest."

"Then you get thirty."

"Talk forty and I'll listen. Who gets the fat end, anyway?"

"That's my business."

"What about my stolen car racket?"

"That's how we screw Liquid again. He'll be counting on continuing running the racket on his new lot, but you tell him you got busted from the Florida end of the operation, and that you're out for good. Then you've screwed him *and* gotten rid of that drain on your numbers income."

"Then who moves my stolen cars?"

"The guy who buys Liquid Yoshu's Sparkling Motors. I'll set that up. Things'll end up the way they were, only with a different mouthpiece."

"Who's the mouthpiece?"

"Guy named Hike."

"*Norb* Hike?"

"You know him?"

"Met him through Liquid a few times. He's a talker."

"Isn't that what you want?"

"I want someone I can trust."

"You can't do worse than Liquid. At least as far as the numbers game goes."

"How do I know that?"

"Hike isn't interested in numbers. He's strictly a used car man. Used cars and worms."

"Worms?"

I pictured Norb Hike on his hands and knees, rolling back a corner of that purple carpeting. "He's got himself a little worm farm."

"There money in that?"

"As much as men like to fish."

"Could me and Hike control that racket?"

I tugged at a chin whisker, remembered Norb Hike's theory about nightcrawlers torn in half. "There are ways to sabotage other farms. That's all I can tell you. You'll have to deal with Hike for details."

Mamma Tar Face's cantaloupe calves lugged her into the room. "When's that Fed bringin' the glue?"

Tar Face put his finger over his lips, waved her away.

The cantaloupe calves disappeared.

"We just might have a deal, Mr. Knuckles. Gimme a day. To think about it."

Scam Eve

Stripping a used car is no easy task. Engines, batteries, generators, brakes, transmissions and front-ends must be removed with the care of a chiropractor.

The evening before The Hard Sell, my father had stripped every car on his lot except a '64 Pontiac. Pam and I had sold the parts off the back of a used pick-up to junkyards and desperate used car owners in the Omaha-Council Bluffs area.

Now the sun was a turnip on the Nebraskan horizon and my father, Pam and I sat on the hood of the good used '64 Pontiac, counting the salad of cash made from parts sales.

Pam's thigh touched mine. Norb Hike's good used '58 Rambler rolled onto the lot. My father looked up from the cash. "What a *run*ner."

The Rambler's door opened. Norb Hike heaved himself out of the plastic-covered driver's seat and stood staring at my father.

My father slid off the Pontiac. "*Son. Of. A. Bitch.*"

Bob Hike shook his bald head, smiling. "You cocksucker you."

They walked toward each other, stopped an arm's length apart, and shook hands. My father yanked Norb Hike's torso toward his, slapped Norb Hike's meaty back. Norb Hike slapped my father's.

Pam had tears in her eyes.

My father pointed to Norb Hike's head, which reflected the red setting sun like a carnival mirror. "Rag top's getting thin."

Norb Hike jabbed my father's waist with an oil-stained finger. "Wish I could say the same for your chassis."

Their grins overflowed onto my face and Pam's. She dabbed her eyes with a yellow toilet paper rosebud: two fathers and forty-three stripped cars were too much for her.

"Got 'em all gutted?" Norb Hike asked.

"All except one," my father said.

"Kid came up with a helluva plan," Norb Hike said, winking at me.

"To marry your catch-of-a daughter?"

"That, too. How *is* my little girl?"

Pam slid off the hood and ran toward Norb Hike. They hugged and she kissed him on his sunset-red forehead.

"How'd you get away from Liquid a day early?" my father asked.

"Used the worm farm excuse," Norb Hike said. Pam's arm was still around him. "Told him I had a gross to sell to a farmer in Adair."

"And he bought it?"

"*Bought* it. You forget who you're talkin' to?"

My father and Pam laughed. I wanted to laugh but still couldn't. I smiled.

"What you say we chow down?" my father asked. "Omaha's got the best beef anywhere. Those stockyards, you know."

Norb Hike picked his nose with his thumbnail. "Steaks sound good."

Squeezing his waist, Pam smiled at me and kept smiling. "Steaks," she said. Her brown eyes twinkled.

"Hey, Romeo," Norb Hike said. "Do me a favor and get that recorder outta my front seat."

"Recorder?" I said.

"Yeah. One of them modern cassette things. Hard to find those used, but I managed."

"Re*cor*der?" my father said.

I slid off the hood.

"And put it in a car next to the one that ain't stripped."

"Recorder," Pam said.

The Hard Sell

There were popcorn clouds in the sky, but the sinkhole seemed hungry for used cars, sifting its way toward demolition of my father's lot and whoever owned it.

My father stood at its edge, chewing cashews. Pam and I stood behind him. "Thing went crazy last night," he said. "Ate the '61 Dodge."

Pam stepped beside him chewing a piece of one of her pink fingernails. "Good thing you guys stripped it."

"True," I said. "But Liquid isn't gonna buy the rest of them, stripped or not, if they're sixty feet under."

"Helps to at least have the chassis there," my father said.

Pam spit some fingernail. "Where's my dad, anyway?"

"I don't know," my father said.

"Got up awful early," I said. "Took that old pick-up and left."

My father watched a piece of popcorn cover the sun. "Got maybe an hour before Liquid gets here." He looked at me, man-to-man. "Got any ideas?"

Pam looked at me also. I looked at the sinkhole. "I'm no geologist," I said, and we all looked at the sinkhole, watching my father's lot go to hell. "Just a used car man."

"Just a used car man," my father said, gazing. "I'm going inside the office. May be my last day to enjoy it."

Pam and I nodded, and he left. I took a step back: the sinkhole was charging. Pam's eyes glistened.

Then something loud and sudden exploded behind the office. Pam grabbed and squeezed my hand. Our eyes met. Her face looked foreign. I turned, yanked away my hand and started for the office, but she grabbed my pants waist and pulled me back. "No."

The office stood there. Norb Hike appeared from behind it, wearing a nail apron and no smile. "GET OVER HERE!" he yelled, and he disappeared behind the office-cabin. "NOW!"

I ran and Pam followed. We rounded the corner of the office. Norb Hike stood near my father's old pick-up. Something very large and flat covered the truckbed.

"Where's my pop?" I asked.

Norb Hike pointed at the large, flat thing.

"What is it?"

"A billboard. I bought it used."

"What was that noise?"

My father appeared from beneath the far side of the billboard. "Backfire from a bad carb. You gonna help lift this? I'll rupture something doing it myself."

I ran to the billboard, grabbed the edge my father was grabbing. Pam and Norb Hike grabbed the opposite edge. What a relief it was, rubbing elbows with my breathing father, looking across at a slick-headed Norb Hike and his sandwich-fresh daughter, holding onto a used billboard like one happy family.

"*Heave*," Norb Hike grunted. Veins surfaced on my father's forehead but seemed to be working: Used billboards are heavy.

We lifted this one off the pick-up. "Back her down," Norb Hike said, and we began walking the billboard to the sinkhole. "Easy," he said. "Incline coming. Got that corner?" His head sweated. "Watch the hole." His nostrils widened. "Now level her out." We began lowering the billboard over the sinkhole. "Use the knees. Think fingers. One. Two. *Three*."

Everyone's fingers were fine. "Hey-hey," I said. "Sinkhole's gone."

The sun slid out from behind a large cloud as my father nodded. "Looks a little suspicious, though, don't it?" He rubbed the back of his neck. "Guess I'll just tell Liquid I was in the middle of painting my own billboard."

"*Oh* no," Norb Hike said. "He's too sharp to buy that." He walked behind the office, returned holding a roll of sod in his arms like a sheep farmer.

Pam, my father and I stood with our mouths open.

"You want me to do everything?" Norb Hike said.

We walked to the pickup, got more rolls of sod, and returned. Norb Hike was on his hands and knees, sodding the billboard. Pam rolled her eyes. "Pull up your pants, Dad."

Norb Hike farted. "Quiet, beautiful."

My father set down a roll of sod, using his knees. "What you pay for these, Hikie?"

Norb Hike began unrolling. "Skinned a construction site

for 'em." His red face glowed like a fire truck. "They paid *me*. Let's get this thing covered. Liquid'll be here in a half hour."

In minutes the billboard was a large advertisement for sod.

Norb Hike frowned. "Sod's a different color than the rest of the lot."

"Like a bad toupé," my father said.

I stepped to the closest gutted car, a '63 Nova, and began pushing it toward the billboard.

Cars roll easily without transmissions.

Norb Hike watched me push. "I like your work."

"Think it'll hold?" my father asked.

I stopped pushing. Pam stepped on the sod and jumped up and down seven times. Norb Hike's lower lip curled over itself. My father nodded.

I pushed the Nova onto the billboard.

"She'll hold another," Norb Hike said. "Hurry."

I pushed a '62 Ford Galaxie 500 onto the billboard. Now the sinkhole was layered deep as a bad childhood memory, with Liquid Johnny due any minute.

My father pointed at his elbow and scratched it. "Remember. Elbow means yes. Shoulder means no."

"Put them sunglasses on," Norb Hike told my father.

"The peroxide!" Pam said.

My father glanced at the sun. "Better hurry."

Pam and I ran to my father's bathroom, where she bleached my hair in hasty, Gertie Hike fashion.

"Don't ever do this to that beautiful brown-paint hair of yours," I said as she towelled my head dry. There was a mirror above the sink: my hair glistened like wet coins.

"We gotta step on it," Pam said, and we ran out of the office. Liquid Johnny wasn't there yet. My father was wearing his mirrored glasses, fluffing his beard with a fistfull of used toothpicks. Norb Hike was getting into his good used '58 Rambler. They waved and we waved back and got in the old pickup. It started. I drove off, took Highway 6 to the bluffs.

I dropped off Pam near the top of a bluff, next to some ditchweed. She began tying a rosary and kissed me through the open window. "Good luck, Blondie."

I sped off, began winding down the bluff to my father's lot. A new jet-black Continental was parked there. Liquid Johnny, in a seersucker jacket, stood outside the log cabin office beside my father, shoulders stiff, hands clasped, black hair slick under sunshine, white teeth flashing.

"You son-of-a-bitch," I whispered as I pulled onto the lot. Liquid Johnny was too busy talking to notice me. I looked at myself in the rear-view mirror. My father shifted an eye out of the corner of his glasses, kept talking to Liquid, touched his elbow.

I got out of the pickup and approached them.

"Mr. Foster," I said to my father.

Liquid Johnny stopped talking.

My father wrinkled his forehead. "Yes, Mr. Sverge?"

Liquid Johnny gave me the once-over, then squinted.

"I'd like to close the deal," I said. I looked at Liquid Johnny's squint, then back at my father's mirrored glasses. "As soon as possible."

Liquid Johnny's inky eyes moved from me to my father like bad penmanship. "This guy looking to buy a car?"

"I'm looking to buy several, sir. I'm looking to buy the lot."

"That makes two of us," Liquid Johnny said. He glared at my father. "You didn't say nothing about another offer."

My father pushed his sunglasses into his nose's red notch. "Mr. Sverge came by just yesterday. I gave you a call but you'd already left Milwaukee."

Liquid Johnny looked at my hair. "Do I know you from somewhere?"

"Maybe. You been to California?"

"Maybe," he said, reading me. "That where you from?"

"Originally. Came to Iowa to buy myself a lot." I sized up the '62 Galaxie 500 on the sodded billboard. "Cars are easy to move here, I heard."

A horn sounded. Norb Hike pulled onto the lot in his good used '58 Rambler, waving and smiling at Liquid Johnny.

Liquid Johnny nodded back. "What part of California?" he asked me.

Norb Hike slammed his car door.

"The eastern part," I said. Sweat moistened my left armpit.

"What city?"

"Los Angeles."

Liquid Johnny cocked his head, pinned my eyes with his. Norb Hike stepped beside him. "Hey Hike, is Los Angeles east in California?"

My father scratched his elbow.

"Dead east," Norb Hike said. There was dirt and nightcrawler slime on his hands. "What is this, a geography lesson?"

"No. But we got ourselves another buyer here. Think they're trying to pull the wool over?"

Norb Hike rubbed nightcrawler slime onto his pant leg. "I guess we'll find out."

"What's with the dirty hands?" Liquid Johnny asked.

"Nightcrawler slime. Just sold another gross a worms."

"That any way to make an impression?"

"No. But I'm sure these men won't mind."

My father smiled. "Not at all, Mike. Was it Mike?"

"Hike. *Norb* Hike."

My father and Norb Hike shook hands.

Liquid Johnny turned to my father. "Keys in all the cars?"

"As ordered."

Liquid Johnny set his palm on Norb Hike's shoulder. "Give 'em the look-see. I've got talking to do."

Norb Hike stepped behind Liquid and walked to the '64 Pontiac. He started it, popped its hood, inspected the only engine on the lot. Liquid Johnny glanced at the rocker panels. Norb Hike's balding head nodded.

Liquid Johnny scowled at me, then turned to my father. "Can we talk alone, Mr. Foster? After all, I made my offer first. And I'm prepared to pay cash."

"If Mr. Sverge doesn't mind."

"I guess it's only fair. As long as I can mention my offer. A hundred thousand. Cash on the barrel head."

Norb Hike slid behind the wheel of the next car over, the stripped '59 Ford I'd hidden the tape recorder in the night before.

My father put his arm around Liquid Johnny's shoulders. "Step this way, partner." They walked to the office like lovers.

Norb Hike held the tape recorder out the Chevy's window. He pushed a button and recorded ignition rang across the lot like wedding bells.

I folded my arms. Norb Hike walked from one stripped car to the next, performed his little inspection act. He wasn't smiling but the slick parts of his head reflected the white Iowa sunshine.

He was playing the recorded idle for the last car, the '63 Nova on the sodded billboard, when Liquid Johnny appeared in the office doorway with an envelope strapped behind the buckle of his alligator-skin belt. My father stepped beside him.

My armpits squeezed sweat from their folds like dish rags.

Norb Hike lifted his pig nose, saw Liquid Johnny, pulled the recorder back through the window, left the tape running.

I walked over to Liquid Johnny, stood between him and the '63 Nova, and frowned. "I suppose you men have made an agreement."

Liquid Johnny gave me his little squint. Norb Hike cut the recording.

"Just about," my father said. "I'm sorry."

Norb Hike walked up, stepped beside Liquid Johnny. "Runners, all of them. Clean little dealership."

Liquid Johnny squinted at Norb Hike. My estimate said he was squinting too much for comfort.

He walked onto the sodded billboard. "If you don't mind, I'd like to . . ." He was reading the '63 Nova as if it were a warning on a box of bad sparklers. ". . . take one of these units for a spin." He slapped the hood and the sound of hollowness made me wince. "Could I take this baby around the block?"

Norb Hike scratched his elbow.

"Go right ahead," my father said.

Norb Hike stared at my father. "Let's take another, Johnny. If he don't have no qualms with this one, why bother?"

"Good thinking, Hike."

"Nothing personal," Norb Hike told my father. "Just being cautious."

"Be as cautious as you want. These cars are as clean as tits in a locked convent."

Norb Hike scanned the lot, nodding like a dashboard doll. When his head stopped, he pointed at the '64 Pontiac. "Let's take that one," he said. He tilted his head toward Liquid Johnny's. "It ran the roughest of all."

They started for the '64 Pontiac.

"Can we chat?" I asked my father, loud enough for Liquid to hear.

"I don't see why not."

Liquid Johnny turned and pointed at the envelope behind his belt. "We'll be right back."

"Swell," my father said. The skin under his beard looked white as condensed milk. Liquid got in the '64 Pontiac. It started, then pulled out of the lot.

"You see a ghost, Pop?"

My father pointed to the sodded billboard. Egg-timer sand action sucked at an edge of the sod. "Gonna swallow the whole works."

"Can't fool Mother Nature," I said, and I walked onto the billboard, to the Nova. "But no one ever said you couldn't hide her for awhile. Wanna give me a hand, Paleface?"

My father and I pushed the Nova from the middle of the billboard to a new and improved spot: on the edge of the billboard, over the corner of the sinkhole's mouth. A breeze blew across Norb Hike's sod job like air-conditioning.

"Just pray he don't notice," my father said.

"He won't if he's in the office."

So we went in the office. My father chewed cashews like piecework. We heard tires squeal and my father swallowed his cashews, then peeked through his dusty Venetian blinds. I peeked also. The '64 Pontiac stood on the sod, where the Nova had been. Norb Hike was behind the wheel.

"Gutsy move," my father said. We quit peeking and he took a form contract off a shelf and sat behind his desk.

I grabbed a pen off the desk, sat on the chair beside it. "Gutsy usually work best."

"Let's hope so."

The door opened. Liquid Johnny walked in. His squint made his face look like yesterday's trousers. Norb Hike stood behind him.

My father handed me the form contract. "I guess it all depends on what these two men have to say."

Clicking the pen, I looked at Norb Hike. His eyes were the size of quarters and sweat curved down the sides of his round head.

Liquid Johnny took the envelope from his seersucker pants waist and glared at my father, then me, then Norb Hike. "Something don't seem right." The envelope trembled. "But maybe it's me." He slapped the envelope on the desk. "Where do I sign?"

My father thumbed through the bills. He pushed Liquid Johnny's contract across the desk top.

Liquid Johnny took a gold pen from inside his jacket, crossed his arms for ten seconds, then signed.

"She's all yours," my father said.

Liquid Johnny smiled. Norb Hike slapped him on the back and I did also. Norb Hike slapped my father on the back and then there was a lot of backslapping and handshaking in general:

"Congratulations."

"Thanks."

"Congratulations."

"Thank you."

"I think we made a square deal."

"Sure enough."

"Sorry I didn't have two lots to sell, Mr. Sverge."

"Don't mind it. That's used cars."

I found myself shaking hands with Liquid Johnny. "You son-of-a-*bitch*, you," I said, wishing I could laugh. "I guess the better man won."

"Sometimes that happens," he said, grinning up a snow-storm. "Tell you what. I saw a hootch store down the road. You guys care to throw back a couple highballs? I'll buy."

The handshakes froze. I looked at my father. "What do you say, Mr. Foster?"

"Highballs it is," he said. "But I buy . . ." He took a crumpled tenspot from his pocket and stuffed it into Liquid Johnny's seersucker pocket. "You fly?"

"Sounds like a winner," Liquid Johnny said. He flashed a blizzard of teeth and walked out the door.

Norb Hike manned the blinds. "As soon as that Conty rounds the corner," he said. "Jesus. He's taking the—"

"The *Pontiac*?" my father said.

The round baldness I'd come to love as Norb Hike's head nodded five times, then froze. His eyes grew wide as sand dollars.

"God damn," he said, grinning. "Look at she *swallow*."

Day Crullers

The Sunday morning smell of fresh crullers on the passenger seat of a good used car might be the best smell ever.

That was the smell I breathed the morning I pulled my good used '52 Volkswagen up the crushed shell driveway, months after Pam, my father and I had moved to the apricot farm in Montana. I didn't know how crushed shells got to Montana, but they were there on our driveway and getting more crushed as I downshifted toward the farmhouse.

On the lawn to my left, a white hen smudged with dirty motor oil pecked at grass sprouting near the flat tire of a '53 Buick, a brown rooster with a cherry-red throat strutting stiffly behind her. On the Buick's windshield was a dusty black and orange FOR SALE sign. The sign was barely visible from the county road but only one or two pickup trucks passed by a day, so that didn't matter.

What mattered was the apricot farm.

Pam was sitting on the second step of the farmhouse porch in her stretchpants, second-hand denim work shirt and thongs, watching me. I pulled on the parking brake, put the white bag of crullers under my arm, and walked up to her, grinning. I pointed at the bag. "Crullers," I said, and I whiffed the scent as it thinned toward the sky.

Pam studied the willow tree near the county road. "There's something I have to tell you."

I sat on that second wooden step, careful not to crush the crullers. Pam's legs were spread the few degrees that pregnancy allows. Her shirt was untucked and unbuttoned twice at the bottom, split over the Ivory-soap-white bowling ball of miniature human being that was making us happy.

But Pam wasn't smiling.

"What is it?" I asked.

She was looking at the bald tire tied to the dock rope

hanging from the lowest branch of the willow. Like crushed shells, dock rope didn't make a lot of sense in Montana, but that didn't matter then.

"Seth's not your father," she said.

The cruller bag fell from my armpit, tumbled down the steps, and lay on the lawn.

"What?"

Pam looked at me more seriously than she had the day we'd thrown the rod in Iowa.

"Seth's not your father. He's not even Seth. He's Donny, an old hitch-hiking partner of your father's who piggybacked one scam on another so he could farm apricots."

Ants crawled over the cruller bag.

"The son-of-a-bitch," I said.

I looked at Pam. Her wet eyes gazed beyond the blue sky, over no rainbow. She pointed to the Ivory bowling ball. "And you're not a father, either."

My jaw fell.

"Donny is."

I pictured three memories: a blind car dealer staring stone-faced at Pam's yanked-down stretchpants, me leaving Council Bluffs after we'd discovered the sinkhole, Pam smiling at every man she ever met—including me.

Then I stood, ran down the stairs, and kicked the cruller bag toward the hanging tire.

Like clockwork, my father or Donny or Son-Of-A-Bitch—who*ever*—opened the cabin door and stepped onto the porch with a baggie of cashews on his palm. He chewed and swallowed a cashew. "Sorry," he said, still chewing. "But your wife and I love each other."

I walked back up the stairs, slapped the baggie off his palm. Cashews seeded the lawn. "You son-of-a-bitch."

Pam stared at the cashews, then winked at Son-Of-A-Bitch and smiled. He smiled back, looked me cold in the eye, and shook his head slowly. Then he burst out laughing, grabbed his stomach, doubled over, and kept laughing, pointing at Pam.

"She sure had you going, Son," he said between laughs, slapping me on the back and laughing harder. "She's a better talker than both of us."

I turned to Pam. She was laughing also, but calmly, her swollen hand steadying the Ivory bowling ball, her eyes twinkling at mine.

My father laughed harder, then coughed out cashew fragments until I returned the back-slapping favor.

"You son-of-a-*bitch*, you," I said.

He held his breath, stopped laughing. His face was red as he touched his wet eyes with his knuckle, and pink as he wiped chewed cashew off his beard with the back of his hand. He pointed to the Ivory bowling ball with the toe of his steel-tipped boot. "Kid oughta be one helluva used car man," he said, and he began giggling.

Pam grinned. "You better believe it," she said. Her grin was contagious, drawing a smirk on the clean slate that had been my face.

Soon she was laughing out loud with my father.

"God help his customers," I said, and I giggled, barely at first but then louder and stronger until all three of our hearts laughed together, our shoulders pumping like pistons in a good used slant-six engine. The hen and the rooster pecked cashews from the green speedometer needles most people call grass, and near the hanging bald tire lay a white bag of crullers: brand new crullers we could whiff, eat, or throw to the sixty thousand bluebirds flying beyond the open sky—if we could just stop laughing.